MW00489886

SPICE ISLAND

A novel

Desert Sands Publishing

Spice Island is a work of fiction. Names, characters, places and incidents are products of the author's imagination or are used fictitiously and are not to be construed as real. Any resemblance to actual events, locales, organizations, or persons, living or dead, is entirely coincidental.

Published by
DESERT SANDS PUBLISHING
PO. Box 6556
Lancaster, CA 93539

Copyright © 2018 by Kimberly Sandhu
Cover: Judi Finnell, https://formatting4u.com

ISBN-13: 978-0-9862514-6-7 (paperback)
ISBN-13: 978-0-9862514-7-4 (ebook)

First Desert Sands Publishing: August 2018

Printed in the U.S.A.
10 9 8 7 6 5 4 3 2 1

ACKNOWLEDGMENTS

To my mother who instilled in me the love of reading and adventure!

Spice Island

The Surgeon and the Sultan

(A Mama's Travel Agency Novel)

Prologue
Washington DC
Late March

*A*ngela

Snow pelted my parka and landed in thick drifts at my feet as I struggled up the stairs from the Foggy Bottom Metro station. Cold, late-season snow blanketed the entire city. My mom's best friend had started a new travel agency, and I'd promised to come out and support the grand opening. If it had been anyone else, I would have passed on this wet excursion through the DC metro system.

My cousin, Queisha, bundled for the weather in a fur coat, red scarf and boots, sloshed besides me as we walked across the street. She complained the entire way. "Angie, I don't see why we have to come out in this mess."

I was resigned to her sour attitude. Quite frankly my mood was not much better. Why did we come out here? Oh yeah, because we would've never heard the end of it if we didn't.

SPICE ISLAND

We worked our way through the crowded afternoon foot traffic, each person bundled and miserable like us. Halfway down the third block, our destination came into view. Sandwiched in between a print shop and bakery, was a door painted in bright tropical colors with letters emblazoned across the front.

Mama's Travel Agency
Call us if ya just gotta go!

"I *really* don't want to do this," I groaned.

Queisha nudged me. "Girl, it's too cold to stand out here complaining. Open it up!"

I peered through the picture window by the door. A warm halo of light filled the space, cozy and inviting. Wind blew an extra helping of snow our way. It swirled around us, collecting at our booted feet. I shuddered. She was right about the cold; but, somehow, I preferred the cold to going inside and facing Janice James, a.k.a. Mama J.

She would hustle me into taking one of her tours. I just knew she would. I couldn't say no because my mother, who was waiting for me, would insist I take the deal. It didn't matter if I was not interested in traveling anywhere. Those two were in cahoots and one way or another they would get me to take a vacation even if it killed me.

I squared my shoulders and opened the door.

Queisha shoved in ahead of me. "You move too slow," she grumbled.

Tropical colors decorated the space. Posters adorned the wall, advertising trips to every corner of the globe, from Tahiti to Tangiers and everything in between. Calypso music played from speakers hidden behind racks full of travel brochures and travel gear. In the middle of the menagerie stood Mama J wearing a bright orange pantsuit and a big grin on her face. "Miss Angela Jones, you finally made it." Leave it to Mama J to make a big deal about my arrival. She pulled me in for a big hug. Her hands wrapped around my back, long fingernails clicked as they met behind me.

My mother, Cora Mae Jones, came from around the desk, wearing a dark blue, wool skirt and sweater combo. Even in this weather, she looked chic and comfortable. She beamed at Queisha and me. "I thought you got lost. We were beginning to get worried."

I gave them a tired smile of reassurance. "With all the weather, there were delays on the metro line."

Mama J didn't miss a beat. "You both made it; that's all that matters." She reached over a table full of suntan lotion. It was stationed near the door and the first thing anyone would see when they walked in. How she expected to sell suntan lotion in this weather was anyone's guess. Her hand emerged with a small travel brochure pressed between her thumb and index finger. "Take a look at this and tell me what you think."

I didn't open it. "This is great, you two," I paused. They stared at me, expectation clear on both their faces. "But, I don't want to go on a Caribbean cruise,"

Mama J clicked her nails. They were an interesting mélange of red, orange and yellow. Only Mama J would try to put a sunset on her long nails. "I thought you would say something like that. You didn't strike me as a Caribbean cruise type." She pointed at the brochure. "That's why you're going to the Serengeti."

"What!" I scanned the contents, panoramic pictures of the African Savanna filled one side of the brochure, animals and safari trucks filled the other. My voice caught in my throat.

Queisha leaned over my shoulder. "A safari, we're going on a safari," she crowed, bouncing on her toes and doing a little dance.

I still did not move. Could not move. Finally, I shook my head. "Mama J, really this is too much. I think I'd rather try the cruise." I handed the brochure back to her but she waived it away.

"I knew you were going to say that. But, believe me, I've picked a great trip for you two!"

My mother stepped over and gave me a squeeze. "Besides, sweetheart, the trip is not until this summer, and Mama J is giving you a special deal. She always picks the best trips for people. You, my dear workaholic daughter, need a vacation away from that damned hospital."

Mama J nodded vigorously. "That's right. You know my motto: *I'ma find you the best trip if ya just gotta go.*"

"But, I don't gotta go!" I protested.

They both chimed in together. "Oh yes, you do,"

Chapter 1
Kariakoo Market
Dar es Salaam, Tanzania, mid-July

*A*ngela

On the first day of our trip to the Serengeti, Queisha and I decided to stay in Dar Es Salaam, the capital of Tanzania, before we began the safari. We went to the Kariakoo Market to buy gifts and souvenirs.

The market spread out before us, a visual feast of people, color and sound. There was so much to see. I stood there mesmerized like a kid in a Halloween candy shop, wishing I could split myself and go in ten different directions at the same time. Shop after shop spilled their wares out onto the sidewalk, everything from clothing and jewelry to spices and produce vied for space and attention.

Queisha nudged me and pushed forward. "Girl, if you don't start moving, we'll never get to the end."

She was right. There was nothing like diving into the fray of shopping to get a girl's motor running, and if I didn't start moving, we would run out of time. At its core, this place was like the Eastern Market back home in DC, a mixture of tourist and residents shopping and haggling for the best deals. There were some differences; speakers blared wonderful East African music, the air was heavier, hotter, a living breathing sauna without an off switch. I fanned myself and began to browse.

We stopped in front of brightly colored t-shirts that hung from a wire strung across the front of a stall. "Queisha, let's get some shirts."

"No, I'm thinking jewelry for my mom." She pointed to the bangles in the shop next door. My cousin loved the shinier things in life, evidenced by her gold nose ring, gold necklaces, and hoop earrings she refused to take off for the safari. She also insisted on wearing her gold-rimmed sunglasses and her gold bedazzled t-shirt with *'I Love Washington DC'* on the front. One look and everybody knew she was American. I cringed. These shop owners were going to have a field day with us.

I had to admit, if only to myself, my mother had been right. I'd needed a vacation. Working crazy hours without a break as a surgeon was killing me. Thanking her with a special gift from our trip was at the top of my to-do list. We reached the end of the street and stopped. The market went on for blocks in every direction. A breeze blew off to my right, and I lifted my face into the wind, grateful for the respite from the heat. "Let's try this way."

Sunlight broke through the clouds and lit the far side of the street illuminating a shop displaying textiles and beads. At the entrance were pieces of fabric swaying in the breeze. One stood out, a jewel sparkling in a sea of cotton. I dragged Queisha past several shops to get a closer look. With a gentle tug, it slipped into my hands. Delicate and finely woven, the material had a bold purple and green geometric border, with a pale lavender flower painted in the central panel. This would be the perfect gift.

"You wanna see more?" The shop owner asked as he stepped out to greet us.

I was so focused on the fabric; his voice startled me. "Um, yes, do you have more of this? Enough to make a dress?"

With eyes sparkling, he gave us a gapped tooth grin. "I have evry'ting. Come inside." His East African accent was thick but understandable.

Queisha groaned. This was not her cup of tea, but she entered the shop with me anyway. Inside, his dark tan shirt and blue jeans stood out against the brightly colored prints we passed. Cloths and textiles were packed tightly together and piled deep on the shelves. Miraculously, he found the exact bolt of material and pulled it out.

"You make good choice." He pointed his stubby finger at the flower in the middle of the image. "Dis iz mikarafuu."

I held it and ran my hands along its length. "What does mikara…what is it in English?"

He cast his eyes toward the ceiling for a moment, then smiled at us. "*Eet* mean cloves in English. *Eet* is our national flower."

Their national flower?

Oh yeah, this really was the piece for my mom. "Do you have someone who sews?"

7

He nodded. "My wife sews. She's in shop next door."

Two women entered, and one loudly called the owner over. Her voice was high pitched, like nails on chalkboard. I shuddered when she called him a second time. He stopped talking to us, quickly moved to greet them and immediately took them to the back of the shop.

Queisha raised an eyebrow. "They must be special clients."

I didn't care, as all my attention was on the cloth. The next thing I knew, the loud heifer pushed me aside and grabbed the bolt of material out of my hand. That's when all the shouting and screaming started.

Queisha moved to intercept her. "Oh no she didn't."

I grabbed her arm. "Wait a second." There was something about the girl that caught my eye.

She was undeterred. "What? Are you going to let that pass? I know we're in a different country, but rude is rude."

"Look at her!"

The rude chick had my five-foot eleven height, same pear shape with generous hips and thighs. Heck, she even walked like me. Not only that, her dark brown hair was braided like mine too. The design was different, but in this Tanzanian heat and the close quarters of the fabric shop, we both had our braids swirled up in a pile on top of our heads. The only difference in our appearance was my soft jeans and t-shirt versus her traditional Tanzanian printed dress.

Queisha stopped in her tracks. Her jaw dropped, and she wagged her finger at them. "Damn, she could be your twin."

I pulled her hand down. "Don't stare."

The girl's companion noticed us. She took the fabric from her to give back to us, but something behind us made her scream. Frightened, she turned to run, accidentally hitting my lookalike in the head with the heavy bolt. She fell against another table of fabric, slipped and landed on the floor disappearing under a waterfall of multi-colored fabric.

What on Earth scared her so?

Behind me, two men holding the largest guns I'd ever seen, muscled their way into the little shop shouting orders in Kiswahili. One fired into the ceiling. Dust and dirt rained down on our heads. Queisha screamed and put her arms up.

I didn't understand what they said but knew standing there like deer waiting to be shot by a hunter was not a good thing. "Get down."

With my heart in my throat, we fell to the floor. Hands grabbed the back of my shirt and pulled me up. I screamed and struck out, hitting one of them in the nose. A large man held me at arm's length to avoid my flailing fists. He possessed corded muscles, thick biceps and hands made to crush rocks. Winning a fight against this guy was impossible, but I was heavier than I looked and had a lot of mass to use against him. I went limp, he lost his grip and let me go. A second man came in to help

9

him. Between the two of them, they hauled me to the door.

Oh. My. God. I'm being kidnaped. Are you freaking kiddin' me?

I swung my legs and arms, determined not to make this easy for them. The men cursed when my hands and feet connected with their flesh. One of the men hit me on the head. The blow stunned me, and the breath whooshed out of my chest. They heaved me onto the back of a truck. Someone covered my mouth and nose with a foul-smelling cloth. The world around me fractured and swirled like a child's kaleidoscope set on low speed.

Lying in the back of the truck, I could feel every rut and pothole straight through to my bones. Even worse, the thick dust caused me to cough and choke, making it impossible to clear my lungs. My ears rang—a high pitch note that mingled with the whoosh of the wind as we sped along. The men's harsh laughter surrounded me, their speech garbled and rough. I had a terrible time focusing, floating somewhere between slightly alert and comatose.

We stopped some time later, my body bruised and battered. I had no idea how long it had been or how far we'd driven. One fact was clear to me—my situation was dire. I was on my own and had to keep my wits about me. I assumed they grabbed me for ransom. If so, they were out of luck. The United States had a no-ransom policy, and my family didn't have money either.

The men jumped out and stepped away, their voices faded in the distance. No one was around making an escape possible. My head was so woozy, the edge of the truck bed looked like it was ten miles away. Undeterred, I pulled myself forward, inch-by-inch closer to freedom. Tears obscured my vision, making it hard to see, but I continued to crawl, drawing closer to my goal. They returned as I flopped out onto the ground.

Damn it; I almost made it.

Someone grabbed me and lifted me to my feet. He held a flask full of some type of liquid. Terror leaped at me, threatening to shut down my mind. I screamed and swung my arms, twisted and turned, but they managed to get enough of the nasty tasting drink down my throat.

What the hell was that stuff?

The world around me shrunk, and my stomach rebelled. My head felt like they'd taken an ax to it. The brew they forced down my throat would come up as liquid fire and drag my beating heart out with it. I was surely about to die.

Hands pulled on the beads threaded through my braids. Some came off, but they pushed them back on. In the far recess of my mind, I thought it was strange they would bother to put beads back in my hair. But, my head was so full of cotton from the stuff they gave me, the thought sifted out almost as soon as it sifted in.

A bearded man, who seemed to be in charge, pulled out a phone, took a picture of me and sent a text. Boy, was he in for a surprise when the person on the other end told him to pound sand. I glared at him, frightened out of my mind, shaking uncontrollably as tears ran down my cheeks,

He said something, his voice raspy.

Was he asking me a question and expecting a response?

The snarl on his face indicated he did. How could I respond? Any second now the entire contents of my stomach would come out and nail him. For some odd reason, the image of his face covered in my vomit paraded across my mind's eye. The stuff they made me drink had me tripping. A hoarse cough escaped my throat; it sounded more like a hollow bark. His hand came at me in slow motion and landed against my cheek. I was so numb at this point, it barely registered, but the force of the slap sent me flying. A cloud of dust and dirt enveloped me when I landed on the ground.

My life had become a welter of images and feeling. The hard crust of the ground as my body hit the rough surface, hands lifting me, men grunting as they carried and tossed me into the truck. Grime filled my mouth and crawled down my throat, threatening to cut off air. I was in hell. Through it all, I cried and chanted to myself, *you must survive. You must get through this.*

The man with the raspy voice leaned over me and raised his hand ready to strike again. I threw my arms over my head in a futile attempt to block the blow as his hand descended...

Chapter 2

*A*mir

The text with her picture came through to my phone. The sun's glare made it difficult to see. I blinked, rubbed my eyes and looked again. It was a picture of Zahra, my fiancée. She was covered in dirt; tears drew muddy streaks down her cheeks, and a purple bruise grew above her right eye. My heart tripped as I gripped the phone tighter. This photo couldn't be real; Zahra was safe in town shopping. My men and I were at the docks unloading the last item from the boat. The sun sat low on the horizon, a flare of light against what promised to be a clear quarter-moon night. The heat of the day faded with the sun, but it was still humid, the air thick with moisture that clung to every inch of my body.

The transfer of goods from the boat had been flawless. Too flawless. I expected an attack, but not a text of Zahra, beaten and bruised.

"Boss, we're done. Let's go." Sidig, my cousin and right-hand man, strode up carrying a duffle bag with the payment from our latest deal. His t-shirt, stained from carrying the cargo of spices and textiles, was plastered to

13

his body with sweat. He never smiled in public, but I could tell by his swagger, he was pleased with the deal. It was his job to make sure all monetary transfers were successfully completed.

I held up my hand for him to wait. "We have a problem."

"That's impossible. I checked and double-checked everything."

I shook my head and showed him the picture on the phone. He hissed, "When did this happen?"

"I don't know." I reread the complete text; there was a number at the end. I pressed, and the call went through.

"This is Amir," I grated between clenched teeth.

The voice on the other end was hard and raspy— *Mustapha*. He was the worst of the worst. If he had Zahra, her life was in danger. I had to act quickly.

"You know who this is?"

"Yes," I growled.

"Then you know I will not hesitate to kill her."

Our enmity was about money and revenge. We had a history that went back a few years. Our businesses had collided dramatically last month. I had expected something would crop up—but not this.

We had a gentleman's agreement to keep family out of our affairs. He'd just crossed the line and I would deal with this breach of protocol later. First, I needed to get Zahra back. I was honor bound to ransom her.

We had an arranged marriage. My father brokered a deal with her father who insisted she be part of the bargain, and I begrudgingly went along with the plan.

The deal was all about the control of territory and political gain. Everything was planned down to the last detail, including the wedding ceremony this weekend. We had not formally met or even spoken to each other. Our engagement was a business arrangement. Business I would not have if this idiot on the other end of the phone killed her. "How much and where shall we meet?"

"Five million, and meet me tomorrow—"

I had to limit her exposure to him, so I cut him off. "If you want your five million, you will have to meet me in thirty minutes."

The silence on the other end of the line was deafening. He was cunning and took his sweet time weighing his options. "You must want her real bad."

I did not answer preferring to let him come to his own conclusions.

"Fine. Five million, cash. Meet me at the main park," his voice grated after a few seconds later.

"No, you meet me at the parking lot near Pier 10," I countered.

He hesitated before continuing. "You have that kind of cash-money lying around?"

I looked down at the bag of money Sidig brought me. Yes, I had cash, but he didn't need to know about it. "You will get a wire transfer. Have your account number ready."

I heard mumbling on the other end of the line. They wanted cash, so it wasn't traceable, but I knew they had clean accounts for these types of transactions.

"Agreed. We meet in thirty minutes."

"Mustapha, not a scratch on her. I mean it."

Thirty minutes later a truck pulled up on the far side of the lot and wheezed to a stop. It was older than dirt and ran on luck because nothing else could hold it together. Mustapha hopped out of the front, alone. This was unusual; he always traveled with a crew. I glanced down the road, a group of men loitered near a building attempting to look inconspicuous. Just as I thought, they were nearby and ready for trouble.

"Let me see her," I demanded.

He raised his hand, and a man in the back sat her up. She seemed dazed but unharmed. I nodded to Sidig, and he stepped over to make the transaction.

I couldn't wait any longer and walked over to the truck. Mustapha tried to block me, but I brushed passed him. She was as limp as a rag doll. Her jeans and yellow shirt were rumpled and dirty. She moaned, turned her head toward me and began to heave. Rage boiled and churned in my gut. How dare he treat her in this manner? "Mustapha what did you give her?"

"Something to calm her down. She was a wildcat."

I clenched my fists. "So, help me if she dies, I—"

Sidig cut me off. "Amir, the transfer is complete."

I reached over and grabbed her, pulling her out of the truck. Mustapha got in and drove off, kicking up a cloud of dust. Rocks peppered us in his wake; I shielded Zahra as best I could. "Zahra, it's okay. I have you." I held her up.

The braids in her hair fell around her soft face, her eyes, a hazel brown, were unfocused. That's odd, the pictures I had of her showed dark brown eyes. "Zahra," I said her name again. She focused on me and promptly threw up. It came up in waves.

I rolled her to the side.

What did they give her?

"Sidig, we have to get her to a doctor."

My cousin was nothing but efficient. Soon, we were at a small clinic, where they saw us immediately.

Zahra kicked and flailed her arms, making it impossible to insert the needle.

"Zahra, stop moving." I kept my voice even and reassuring, even though I was mad as hell and concerned for her survival. I wanted to yell at someone, anyone, but knew it would not help this situation.

She moaned and writhed as I struggled to restrain her. My God, this whole experience must have terrorized her, and here I was making it worse by holding her down so he could treat her. When the doctor inserted the needle in her arm, she flinched and cried out. Once the fluids reached her system, she calmed down and seemed to be over the worst of it.

She needed to go home and rest. I pulled out my cell and punched in her father's number. It rang and rang until it switched over to the answering system. I hung up, not sure how to explain Zahra's kidnapping and her current comatose state. I looked at her lying there on the bed. She was pale and bruised. This was definitely an in-person kind of discussion, not the type of information to leave on an answering machine.

Against custom, and all kinds of decorum, I decided to take her to my private home on an island, far away from prying eyes. We could not afford for anyone to see her like this and in the presence of a non-male family member.

Sidig and I whisked her away on our boat. She didn't wake as I carried her up from the pier to my room. I had my female servants change her and place her in bed. Once they were gone, she began to, toss and turn. She was supposed to be fine, the doctor assured me, but something was wrong. Seeing her like this was intolerable. Out of desperation, I dashed to the bathroom and found a towel, splashed cool water on it, returned to her side and dabbed it on her forehead. It helped a little, but she continued to writhe and moan.

I had no experience in comforting a sick person and was not sure what else to do. Getting in the bed to hold her was out of the question. We were not officially married. But…she looked so worn out and miserable. Her forehead creased in pain, and her eyes pinched closed; half-moon shadows spread out and marred her unblemished skin. She rolled to her left, then to her right. I glanced at the closed door. No one would know if I spent a few moments holding her.

Just a few minutes to calm her down. What's the harm in that? After all, we're engaged.

I sat on the bed next to her and scooped her up. She continued to shake but seemed content letting me wrap my arms around her shoulders. I rubbed her back, and slowly, she stopped moving, took a deep breath and settled down. She even threw her arms around me, nuzzling her soft curves into me. She felt good. I began to think this arranged marriage would not be so bad after all. "Do you feel better?"

Those beautiful, hazel eyes focused on me. "Hmm?"

I whispered her name, "Zahra."

She mumbled something, shook her head, closed her eyes and fell asleep.

I lay there all night and late in the morning holding her. This was something I'd never done with a woman. Female entanglements were too costly in this part of the world. What comfort I found usually happened abroad, and I never lingered and held the woman. But there was something about her that made me want to hold and protect her.

I lifted her hands; they were long and graceful. I wondered what she did with them in her everyday life. And, her eyes, the two glimpses I had of them showed deep amber pools of intelligence and grace. She was someone I could hold a long conversation with early in the morning after a night of...

I stopped myself and got serious. This arranged marriage was a business deal and nothing more. But still, maybe I could hope for more.

The sun was high in the sky when my phone rang. Maybe this was her father. I slipped off the bed and went into the hallway to take the call.

Chapter 3

*A*ngela

A phone rang, the tone a soft melody that sounded familiar, but my brain was so full of cotton, I couldn't place it. The bed shifted, and a few seconds later, a door opened and closed. I lay there for a moment, then sat straight up.

Where the hell am I?

The terror I felt earlier slowly began to reassert itself. I drew in my knees and began to shake.

My head ached; I massaged my temple, grasping desperately for the last few details of my life before I blacked out. I recalled a man grabbing me and pulling me out the truck. I threw up. All of my anguish, fear and frustration came out in one sickening heave along with my breakfast. My lunch came out in the second go around, most of it landed on his face and chest. Strangely enough, he did not push me away. Instead, he pulled the braids from my face and held me as I continued to empty the contents of my stomach. His touch was gentle. He even rubbed my back and said something to me. I didn't understand him, but the sound of his voice was soft and soothing.

The next thing I remember was a boat ride, I think, and then someone gently cradled me in his arms and carried me upstairs. My mind stuck on this one impressive fact because no one I knew could carry me. Not even the guy who grabbed me in the fabric store could hold me. I have not been picked up since I was four-years-old. At five feet eleven inches tall and a good size fourteen, if I wore spanks, the odds of someone lifting me were like a zillion to one. I decided my mind must have slipped from the haze of drugs, and I made up the part about a man picking me up and carrying me.

I glanced down, my jeans and t-shirt were gone replaced by a colorful kaftan, my skin had the lingering scent of soap instead of vomit.

Someone had bathed me and removed my soiled clothes.

There was nothing more unnerving than the realization that a chunk of my life was missing from my memory, even more so, the fact that I was in a strange place wearing a strangers' clothes. *Frightening* was the word that came to mind. My breath turned into short agonizing gasps and raced ahead of my galloping heart. I hid my face in my hands and let out a sob, draining the emotion from my system; then, I released a shuddering breath. Hysterics were not going to help me in this situation. I had to remain calm and think clearly.

I was in a man's bedroom by the look of it, all brown tones, leather chairs and dark wood. They'd put me in the

21

middle of a comfortable king-sized bed, covered with deep purple, satin sheets infused with the scent of cinnamon and vanilla spice. I ran my hands across the smooth material, cool to the touch.

The large room had two sets of French doors opening onto the most amazing view of a garden and lagoon complete with palm trees and tropical flowers. A bright blue sky dotted with clouds served as a backdrop. Palm trees swayed in the breeze and a lone wind chime rang musical notes through the air.

How did I go from a dust-covered truck and crazed insurgents to a resort?

My right arm stung, someone had attached a Band-Aid in the crook of my elbow. I pulled it off exposing a pinprick of blood. *What did they do to me?* My hands shook, my pulse picked up speed again. *Did they take me to the doctor and treat me?* I vaguely remembered a clinic, but the memory was hazy, like a cool, ocean mist drawn in watercolor, fuzzy and indistinct.

I was alone for now and could run without anyone to stop me, but a sudden urge to pee interrupted my train of thought. I crawled out of bed and went straight to the bathroom.

Odd, how did I know this door led me there?

After relieving myself, and, oh heaven that felt good, I walked across the room and stepped outside onto the terrace. A garden full of tropical flowers spread out in front of me. There was a fountain at the far end, water trickled over stones and splashed into a pool at its base. Farther out was a lagoon with a small boat tied to a pier.

A sweet scent of spices hung in the air, lending a sense of peace to the area.

I looked left then right.

Where were the bad guys?

There was no one to stop me from taking the stairs that led down from the patio, run to that boat and escape. Muffled chatter of female voices and laughter came from the other side of the door. People were coming. My heart tripped.

Okay, girl, flight or fight. Which one will it be?

The voices were closer, now. My body was moving, even before I formed the thought. They would have to catch me first. I bolted like a rabbit.

Feet don't fail me, now.

I flew down the path leading to the small dock, aiming straight for the boat tied there. A cry went out; a woman on the terrace pointed at me. I put on more speed.

"Zahra," a man's voice called out.

Was he telling me to stop? Is that what that word meant?

Heavy footsteps thumped behind me.

"Zahra!"

I glanced back and stumbled in shock. The most gorgeous man I had ever seen was running after me. His body was lean, muscled and tan. He ran like an Olympic sprinter, long legs, graceful strides and fast.

My adrenaline kicked into high gear, and I ran a little faster chastising myself every step of the way. Mr. Fine-as-wine was chasing me, and I'd just jeopardized my life and limb to give him a second look.

Keep moving Angela, don't let a good-looking face and hot body stop you from escaping.

He said other words in Kiswahili that could just as well have been said in Greek for all I understood. The boat was tied near the end of the pier. My feet made a low thumping sound as I slowed long enough to unloop the rope from the bollard and step off. He caught me in mid-stride and pulled me back. I screamed and swung at him. He ducked and caught my wrist.

"Get away from me!" I yelled pulling out of his grasp and stomping on his foot.

"*Ahrggg,*" He hopped on one foot while rubbing the other.

A pair of oars were stacked on the pier. I grabbed one and swung around. He lowered his foot, ducked away, and put his hands up, a confused look spread across his face. As for me, I was completely out of breath and wheezing…a lot. That last burst of speed did me in. But I'd be damned if I go down without a fight. I swung the oar at him. "I demand to be released."

He took two steps back and stared at me. "You speak English." He paused and said the next few words in amazement, "Like an American." Slowly he put his hands down, cocked his head to the side and studied me from head to toe as if I was some sort of alien.

"That's because I am one." I menaced him with the oar and continued to move back toward the boat.

"No, wait."

"Why? So you can keep me captive forever?"

"But—"

"No buts, mister. I'm out of here." I swung the oar at him like it was an oversized baseball bat. My foot grazed the edge of the pier, a quick glance revealed I was nowhere near the boat.

Damn.

"Listen to me. It's not safe," he warned.

There was something in his tone that gave me pause. "What do you mean?"

"The last board is loose. You must move away."

"What?"

Suddenly, a terrible cracking sound came from the board. One minute I was standing on wood, the next, I was standing on air. My arms windmilled, and the oar sailed away. He reached me a second too late and we both fell. His hands circled my waist and he turned us so he would hit the water first to cushion me from the impact.

My skin instantly pebbled from the cold shock of water as it closed over our heads. His arms enclosed me like a protective cloak. Instinctively, I held my breath, but everything happened so fast, I inhaled water and retched. His dark gaze never left my face, and he saw me gag. We touched bottom, he bent his knees and pushed off with so much force, we broached the surface in less than a few seconds. I coughed and sputtered attempting to clear my lungs. He tightened his arm over my diaphragm and more water than I cared to think about came out of my mouth.

Gently, he gathered me close and used his right hand to pull us toward the shore. He kicked slowly, his legs tangled with mine giving me a hint of their hard angles and strength. His smile exposed a row of perfect teeth. "I think there has been a mistake." His accent was melodic with a slight British clip.

I held on to him like he was a rescue float, too weak to kick or do much else. "Ya think?"

His looks, his smile, even his calm demeanor completely disarmed me. He was so different from the men who grabbed me. Questions tumbled through my mind as he pulled us along. How did I get here? Was he involved with the kidnappers? Did he hire them? I needed answers.

We reached the shallow part of the surf where I could stand. But as soon as my feet touched solid ground, he swooped me up in his thick, muscled arms and walked out of the water. He held me with no effort at all; my weight did not bother him a bit.

"No," I bunched up in a vain hope this position would lower my mass. He ignored me, calmly carrying me to a small, wooden boardwalk and set me on my feet as if I was a delicate teacup. I shook uncontrollably and clung to him unable to let go. He was in his mid-thirties like me, over six feet tall, broad shoulders, smooth skin and lots of hard muscles. Holding him was like holding onto the side of a mountain, a man-mountain.

Our eyes were inches apart; his lips hovered close to mine. I was frozen in space and time, unable to move away or closer. Firmly he placed his hands on my waist and pushed away, widening the gap between us, breaking the spell. For surely only a spell would explain why I was unable to move or speak. My voice was gone, lost somewhere in the addled recesses of my brain. I had one conscious thought swirling around in my skull and it involved touching him to verify if he was real.

He placed his hand over his heart and bowed in greeting. "My name is Amir Bin Abdul Bin Sultan,"

I worked my throat and swallowed once praying my voice would sound normal. "I'm Angela Jones," I breezed.

Angela, girl that came out waaay to breathy. Get a grip.

He gave me a thousand-watt smile. If I was confused before, his smile just scrambled my brain and served it for breakfast. Up close, this man was delicious. His smooth bronze skin, dark curly hair that now glistened with droplets of water was oh so nice. His smile was full of perfect teeth, framed by a neatly trimmed beard.

"Welcome, Angela Jones, to Spice Island."

With his accent, my name came out sounding exotic. The beginning had rounded tones like 'Ahn' and finished off with a soft 'j' in 'gela.' I really liked hearing him say my name.

He motioned toward another man who approached the dock.

"This is my cousin, Sidig."

His cousin bowed in greeting. He was swarthy, yet his features were Arabic. He wore a loose-fitting, tan shirt and pants that flowed around him as he moved.

To the depths of my soul, I should've been furious about everything that'd happened to me. But, I stood

27

there feeling, safe…maybe? I had to get it together and take stock of my situation. First things first. He said we were on Spice Island. That told me a lot. "Um, I've never heard of this place." I swallowed. My mouth still felt like cotton.

"You know it as the island of Zanzibar," he responded.

It must have taken me too long to process this information because he pointed out to sea. "It's off the coast of Tanzania. Dar es Salaam is that way."

I finally got my wits about me, stood straighter, lifted my chin and nodded. "Thank you. Now, please return…" I stopped in mid-sentence. His eyes scanned me from head to toe. These were eyes of a hungry man.

What the hell now?

I glanced down. *Oh, gag me!* The kaftan they'd put me in clung to every gracious curve God gave me. To make matters worse, the damn thing was transparent when wet, and I had nothing on under it.

Oh, horror!

And, there I was standing in front of two men on display like Botticelli's Venus stepping out of a clamshell.

I quickly wrapped my arms around my chest, not believing for a second this simple move would help a thing. My God, his cousin was standing behind me. Lord above, the view he was getting must have sizzled his eyes.

Amir's gaze met mine. He understood my embarrassment and pulled me into his arms. In a flash, he turned and shielded me from his cousin and the woman approaching from the far side of the garden. She must have been a servant, because he said something to her, and she returned to the house.

He translated for me, his deep voice made something inside of me uncoil and sit up in complete attention. "I asked her to get a robe for you."

The minutes dragged, hard muscle and bone held me tight. Heat from his body baked into me like an oven. All I needed to do was turn my buns around to finish the job. Done. Cooked to perfection.

I couldn't move though, didn't want to move, our lips were mere inches apart. He smelled like the island, cinnamon and spice, with a touch of musk added on for extra measure. My head swam. The urge to close the gap and taste those full lips was strong. I hung there, suspended in time.

I used to fight with myself in these situations. I have a rational side I call, 'Rational Angela,' then I have the naughty street side of me, I call, 'DC Angela.'

Standing there, hugged up against Amir, released DC Angela from the jail cell Rational Angela stowed her in. The cell door clanked open and DC Angela came out roaring.

Go on, kiss him!

Rational Angela sat on my right shoulder, large and in charge, whispering in my ear.

Ignore her and back away.

She was correct; I needed to back away. But, before I moved, DC yelled, *look up*. I lifted my gaze to meet his dreamy, bedroom eyes. Almost black and framed with long lashes, they were dark, exotic and seductive. Images of hot, sweaty Arabian nights crowded my brain and drowned out the wails of Rational Angela.

Oh, the things I could do with this man. I closed the gap, one inch. I swear I felt a low predatory growl rumble from deep in his chest. He moved closer...

"Ahh-hmm..." Somewhere behind Amir, his cousin coughed. We both jumped.

Amir pulled away from me and gave his cousin a look that could kill a thousand lions. My mind cleared, like the sun cutting through fog.

Was I about to kiss this man?

I pulled farther away. Rational Angela was cheering; DC Angela was in full revolt. She was out of her cage and on the prowl. There would be a war between these two, with lots of blood and gore on the ground.

What *was* I thinking? I lowered my eyes. The traditional long, white cotton shirt he wore fell to his knees, wet from our dunk in the lagoon. He also wore tan pants that clung to his legs and revealed sweet heaven. Well-cut abs tapering into a tight waist with thighs that could crack nuts, and oh, yes, a healthy bulge between those thighs.

Amir's cousin cleared his throat again, and I brought my errant eyes up to meet Amir's. Jesus, he *knew* what I was thinking. His lips were raised in a crooked grin. His eyes were hooded and burned a hole straight through to my soul.

Okay, I was busted. It was time to stop studying him. Logical Angela took over completely and lectured me about thinking of ways to escape instead of ways to have an escapade.

His cousin said something, and Amir glanced back, shook his head and turned to focus on me.

And. He. Was. Focused.

He had the look of a hungry but irritated man. For a hot second, I thought his irritation was because his cousin was there, and he would prefer to be alone with me. His arms snaked around me again caging me in to keep me all to himself and not solely to protect me from his cousin's gaze.

Keeping me to himself?

I must have lost my mind. These men may have been involved in my kidnapping. They were going to get a lot of lip from me about this unpleasant fact as soon as I got some less revealing clothes on.

A quick glance over Amir's shoulder told me his cousin was amused by this turn of events. The guy said something and stepped aside to allow an elderly lady to pass. Her iron-gray hair accentuated mahogany skin. She gave me the sweetest smile that reminded me of my grandmother. The blue robe she carried matched her flowing dress. Amir held me for a few more seconds, then slowly stepped away to allow her to cover me.

"*Ahnjela*, this is Maritsa. She will take you back to my room and see to your needs."

Maritsa quickly bundled me up in the robe and hustled me up the wooden path back into the house, clucking like a mother hen. Before I stepped in, I looked back. Amir was still gazing at me, completely ignoring his cousin who was talking and waving his arms in a vain attempt to get his attention.

Chapter 4

*A*mir

Standing there dripping wet, with a silly grin on my face made me look like a fool, but I could not help myself. The memory of her lavender and jasmine scent lingered in the air. Her spirit was as hot as the summer sun, the kind of heat that burned down to the bone and left a deep rich tan in its wake. Her voice a sirens' song, smooth as the zephyr wind flowing in from the sea. Every inch of me vibrated and hummed, a finely tuned sitar ready to be strummed and plucked by the musician. Angela could play me all night long, and I would use Persian poetry for the lyrics.

Sidig tried to get my attention. His hand flickered in front of my face like a fly. I fanned it away refusing to take my eyes off her until she was back in my room. One short encounter and Angela had taken the breath from my body and set my soul ablaze.

"Amir, pay attention." Sidig's irritation wound itself through to my brain.

I straightened up and turned toward him. He pulled out the cell phone and handed it to me. "You have to call Chief Bintu back."

"Who?" The woman must have scrambled my brain because it took me a couple of seconds to remember Bintu was her father. No. He was Zahra's father. My eyes opened wide. "If she is *Ahnjela*, then where is Zahra?"

He pointed at the phone. "That's what I came down here to tell you. Chief Bintu wants you to call him back. He has been at the hospital all night long with Zahra. That's why you couldn't get him earlier. It seems she was shopping in town when men attacked the store. She fell and got a concussion."

I nodded and dialed the number. "Bintu, this is Amir. How is Zahra?"

"She's fine," his gruff voice answered.

Zahra's injury was a good excuse to delay the wedding. I stole a glance in the direction of my room. To be honest, I wanted to delay the wedding indefinitely. "Sidig told me she was injured. Let's move the wedding date to next month,"

"Absolutely not! The deal must be finalized this weekend," he yelled so loud I had to move the phone away from my ear.

"There'll be serious repercussions if you back out," he finished.

Oh yeah, he was determined to have Zahra married off, and the business with my father wrapped up by Sunday afternoon.

"But, what about Zahra? Will she be well enough?"

"Don't worry about her. She'll be there." He was firm in his declaration.

I suspected he would drag her to the ceremony while she was still in the hospital bed. "Fine, then we'll see you this Sunday." Arguing would only serve to agitate him more; I acquiesced simply to get him off the phone.

Sidig listened to the whole conversation, and his smirk spoke volumes. "Don't give me that look."

"What look?"

"That amused, how did he get himself into this predicament, look."

He followed me back to the house. "Oh, *that* look."

I swear some days I could freely throttle my cousin. "What was I supposed to say? I ransomed the wrong woman; she is currently in my room, and the wedding is off?"

A crooked grin spread across his face. "Does that mean you like our American?"

"No," I lied.

He was right. I liked her. One look, and I was hooked. Logically, I knew she belonged to another world far removed from this island. She had survived a horrible ordeal and would want to go home. But, I wanted to keep her here, to get to know her. What did she like? What made her laugh, or more importantly, how could I please her?

Deep in the interior of the house was a courtyard that was open to the sky. I always found my way to this space when I needed to think. In the far corner, chairs were placed under a sunshade. I pulled one out into the sun. My clothes were mostly dry; another few minutes in this heat would finish the job.

Sidig ambled up and sat across from me. He pushed his sunglasses up and leaned back. "You can't keep her here."

I rolled my eyes. "Don't you think I know that?"

He shrugged his shoulders. "Thought it needed to be said, that's all."

Maritsa entered with a tray of tea. She gave me a rather pointed look, quietly set it down and left. The tea settled me enough to remember what troubled me. "Sidig, they kidnapped her for a reason."

He smirked as if the answer was obvious. "Yeah, to get money out of you."

I shook my head. "It was more than that. I'm sure of it." The whole scenario played for the hundredth time in my head. Mustapha agreed to a wire transfer instead of cash much too quickly. It was almost as if he wanted us to take her as soon as possible. And, why did he drug her? What was his angle in all of this?

Sidig tensed and leaned forward. "You don't think it's because of the shipment you stole from him? There's no way he could've found out it was you."

"I know... but something is not right." I waved my hand in the direction of my room. "

Now, I have a woman in my bedroom who should not be there."

Angela

A hot shower was in order after my unplanned plunge into the lagoon. I was frustrated, wet and still a captive. The bathroom was a palace, almost as large as the bedroom itself. This time, I had a chance to get a good look at it. Everything was tiled in jewel tones and clear glass, and to top it all off, the sink was gold. Was I in a gilded cage? I stopped at the sink and stared into the mirror.

"How did you end up in this predicament, Angela?"

My image did not reply, thank God. If it'd answered, I would've run to the hills screaming. My reflection looked decidedly sad. The bruise above my right eye was a mottled purplish color. I gently touched it and winced. It hurt like hell. At least I didn't have a hard knot rising under it. The braids were wet, limp and pulled at the more tender sections of my scalp. I touched one spot where they hit my head the day before. It hurt like the devil too.

I needed to inspect it, so the braids had to go. The process of pulling and unbraiding was fairly easy. I had had the sense to get a design that was easy to take out. To contain the beads, I grabbed a small decorative bowl from the shelf. They made a soft clunk as I deposited them one by one. Some missed the bowl, clattered onto the counter then rolled off onto the floor to disappear under the cabinet.

Soon I was able to check my scalp. I'd probably have a headache for the next few days, but I would live. One hot shower later, and I was ready to tackle the world. My head was clearer, and I was focused. Maritsa had left a dress and taken the wet one away. I had no choice but to put it on. I liked the color; a bold orange and red print scarf layered over a lemon yellow dress that buttoned underneath my bosom. Not something I would usually wear. I was normally self-conscious about accentuating my bosom and always found clothes to de-emphasize them.

I didn't even try to tame my hair. Wet curls ran riot all over my head, they bounced and dripped water as I swung into the hallway. Maritsa was waiting for me. She smiled and pointed to the right. I squared my shoulders and marched into battle ready to give Amir a piece of my mind.

He and his cousin were in an intense conversation when I entered the patio. Amir abruptly stood to greet me. He moved a bit too fast though, and a tray of tea tumbled to the floor. It made a racket that bounced and echoed off the walls.

These guys had me kidnapped?

This did not compute.

"Please, come and sit down." Amir pointed to a comfortable patio chair.

I was ready to come in and give him a piece of my mind until my eyes focused on his. The memory of his arms wrapped around me came roaring back with a vengeance. I could feel his body infusing me with the heat of ten suns. I flushed, sat down and concentrated on maintaining a steady voice. DC Angela, on the other hand, was panting. I swear that girl was going to get me into a lot of trouble. "Am I being held captive?"

"No, not at all." His voice vibrated right through me and straight into my bones.

His answer surprised me. I was expecting an argument and not a sincere look of regret. I forged on. "Then I can leave?"

He nodded. "Yes, of course."

Was I hearing him correctly? It could not have been this easy. Maritsa arrived with fresh tea and a new tray. She cleaned up the old mess and handed me a cup of chai.

His cousin stood up. "I must attend to a few matters."

I held my hand out. For the life of me, I could not remember his name. "Wait, what's your name again?"

"Sidig." He gave a slight bow, smiled and left.

"I'm sorry you were taken," Amir said.

He seemed so sincere. But, this did not excuse the fact I was on the Island of Zanzibar and not on my safari. Hell, after everything that had happened to me, my preference would be to run home and hide. "Did you have me kidnaped?"

He shook his head. His hair shifted in a cascade of curls around his head. My eyes watered and I took a long drag on the tea. I had to admit that it was good, but looking at him was better.

39

"I didn't have you kidnapped. Apparently, you were mistaken for my fiancée. A competitor of mine kidnaped you for ransom."

I was the wrong girl? This man paid a ransom for me? These little tidbits were secondary to the news he had a fiancée. "You're engaged to be married?"

Now, why did that come out of my mouth?

"Yes, the wedding was to be this weekend. It may be delayed now."

He was hedging. "It *was* scheduled for this weekend? What happened?"

"It seems my fiancée, Zahra, was knocked down when they grabbed you. She suffered a concussion and is now in the hospital."

I put the cup down. Zahra must have been that rude girl in the store. My doppelganger. "I am so sorry to hear that. Is she okay?"

"Yes, she'll make a full recovery."

Something was not right about this whole situation. If he was engaged, why did he think I was his fiancée? "Why couldn't you tell I was the wrong person? We don't look that much alike, do we?"

"Actually, you do."

I raised an eyebrow.

"Well, to be honest, I've never met her face to face."

"What? How's this possible?" I enunciated each word, completely baffled by his statement.

He shrugged. "It's an arranged marriage. We were to meet for the first time this weekend."

I had heard of these arranged marriages, but never thought I would meet someone tangled up in one. "Oh, I see." I really didn't see but hey, different strokes. I was more concerned about getting him alone. I mean… getting home. Oh, my Jesus, I was losing it, plain and simple. The bump on my head had addled my brain.

Refocusing on the situation I remembered Queisha. "I need to call my hotel and check on my cousin. She was with me, and I have to make sure she's okay." Even if she was okay, I was pretty sure she would be completely freaked out over my disappearance.

Amir pulled out his phone. "Yes, of course. What's the name of your hotel? I'll call right away."

A few minutes later I was speaking with Queisha.

"Oh, my God, Angie; are you okay?" Queisha was understandably upset. She saw them hit me and throw me into the truck.

"Yes, I'm a little sore but fine."

"Where are you?"

I modulated my voice hoping a calm response would settle her nerves. "I'm somewhere on the island of Zanzibar,"

"Zanzibar? How did you get there?"

"A guy ransomed me and brought me here." I realized this was the wrong thing to say to my man-hungry cousin.

Her voice rose two octaves. "What? How did that happen?"

This line of questioning would be better discussed in person. "Queisha, listen to me. I'll explain everything

41

when I get there." I put my hand over the receiver. "Amir, how long will it take to get me back to the mainland?"

"Sidig left to go and call the boat. We're on the far side of the island, and it's about a four-hour ride. You should be there by the evening."

I relayed the information to Queisha. "Don't worry; I'll see you soon," I added, praying everything went as planned. I'd had enough trauma to last me a lifetime.

"Okay, but be safe, Angie; you scared me half to death,"

I handed the phone back to Amir. "Thank you."

He gave me a thousand-watt smile that melted my bones. "You're welcome. I'm truly sorry for the mix-up. Please have a late lunch with me before you go."

Now, what is a girl to do? Say no to a gorgeous man's lunch invitation?

 I nodded.

Amir stood up and motioned for me to follow. "This way. The terrace by the room has the best view on the island."

Chapter 5

*A*ngela

The terrace was straight out of Aladdin's storybook. A half-round balcony complete with an ornate ironwork railing overlooked gardens that fanned out below. Flowers bloomed, golden yellow, purple and orange, an exotic variety to keep a botanist happy for years. Beyond the garden, palm trees swayed in a light breeze as the scent of spices infused the air. This was a lovely place for a meal.

In the center of the terrace was a round table with two chairs. There were also two place settings for an intimate lunch. A small fountain trickled in the corner; water splashed and sparkled in the afternoon sunlight.

The view drew me to the rail. Amir joined me, and we watched the garden in an awkward silence. My first instinct was to lean into his warm goodness, but I pinched myself and stood still. There was relative safety in small talk, so I filled the void with light conversation. "Your garden is beautiful."

"Thank you. My father had it planted for my mother."

"That's so sweet."

His smile didn't quite reach his eyes. "When my mother passed away, my father moved back to the capital, Muscat, and left the house and gardens to me."

"I'm sorry about your mother."

His face was etched with sadness as he turned and waved toward the table. "Come, have a seat."

He held a chair out for me. Once I was settled, he poured tea for us both and continued. "She passed away a few years ago. How about you? Are your parents still alive?"

"Yes, my father is in New York, and mother is with me in Washington D.C."

He leaned back, the sun glinted off the glass in his hand. "They're not together?"

"No, and it's a long story." I would not, could not, elaborate on the sorry tale of my parents. Besides, I was more interested in what he did in life. He said his father was from Muscat. "Isn't Muscat the capital of Oman?"

"Yes, we're Omani."

I remembered what I'd read about Oman's long history with Zanzibar. The Sultanate had a lot of holdings down here. "Are you related to the Sultan?"

He nodded. "I'm his youngest son from his third wife."

Wow, I did not see that coming.

"What does a Sultan's son do for a living?"

He gave me a strange look. "I sell spices for the family company."

Zanzibar, in its heyday, was the center of trade for spices, but that was over four hundred years ago. They still sold spices but in smaller volumes. Never thought I would meet the owner of a spice company though. Much less one that had enemies who wanted to harm his fiancée.

"Very interesting. This seems like a benign job…"

He put the glass down and shifted his weight. "It is."

I wasn't sure how to express my thoughts, but I continued, "Then why would a rival in the spice industry want to kidnap your fiancée?"

His answer was interrupted by Maritsa's arrival with a platter full of food. Sidig paced behind her, carrying a carafe of wine. He spoke to Amir, then quickly stepped into the room. Speakers, hidden behind the door, soon filled the air with the soft strains of music. My head bobbed back and forth in time with the beat. "It's a Jazz quartet. Good choice."

Amir leaned forward. "Maritsa insisted. She wants you to have a pleasant meal before you go." He picked up the carafe and poured. "Try this. She makes it from the fruit she harvests from our garden."

It was wine but like nothing I'd ever tasted before, light, fruity and fresh. One sip quickly turned into four. "Hmm, it's good. My compliments."

"I'll let her know you like it."

We both filled our plates with a large helping of lamb, rice and vegetables. It tasted as good as it smelled, and soon we were eating and talking like we knew each other for years.

"What do you do for a living?" Amir asked.

"I'm a surgeon at a hospital in Washington D. C."

Amir stopped, put his fork down and scooped my hands into his. He caressed them, running the pads of his fingers over every inch, feather-light, gentle. "Your hands are beautiful. I knew you did something special with them."

I wasn't sure what to say. He had a strange look in his eyes as he studied them. I finally decided the easiest reply would be a polite one. "Um, thank you."

There it was again, the man, the heat, the intense desire to throw myself into his arms. I was suddenly glad there was a table between us. He rubbed my hands again then placed them on the table.

The music changed to a song I recognized. "Is this... a Queen song?"

Amir nodded. "Yes." He stood up and offered his hand.

The man danced too? Be still my heart.

He pulled me up into his embrace. Right there in the middle of a terrace overlooking a beautiful garden on Spice Island, we danced to the song *Crazy Little Thing Called Love.*

He twirled me around, held me close and twirled me again. Between the wine and the spins, I was not sure if I was dancing on a tiled terrace or on a cloud. My goodness, the man had moves. Soon enough, a slower song came on. Also, by Queen.

I wondered why he had this music. It was a complete departure from the Tanzanian music I had heard in the market or even the jazz he'd played earlier. "Not that I mind, but why Queen?"

He laughed and swung me around again. "Freddie Mercury, their lead singer, was from Zanzibar.

I stopped mid-spin. "No way."

"Yes way. I love their music." His smile was open and genuine.

I gave him my most beguiling look. "Are you allowed to dance like this with a woman?"

He pulled me in tight, brought his cheek to mine and whispered in my ear, "No." His breath tickled. "I can't help myself. I'm under your spell."

My voice hitched, and I swallowed the lump in my throat. There was nothing much I could do with my runaway pulse.

He shifted his head bringing his lips closer to mine. My heart hammered; heat rose in shimmering waves. Beads of moisture edged my temples and other naughty spots. I was sweating like a sinner in church.

And. This. Man. Was. Sin.

Sex, sin and all the sweet memories that would come with it.

His lips brushed mine. "Tell me not to kiss you." He paused. "If you let me kiss you, I may never stop."

DC Angela kicked Rational Angela off my shoulder. Poor girl landed on the floor and was out for the count. I nodded and brushed my lips against his.

Sweet, treasure.

His lips molded over mine, our tongues tangled. The kiss was commando, and so hot it burned the alcohol out

47

of my system and launched me into the sky. I did not want him to ever stop. He pulled me in closer, and I felt every hard muscle he owned, especially the one in his crotch.

I vaguely heard a phone ring, then footsteps approaching fast. "Amir," Sidig called.

Slowly he pulled away. Our eyes were locked as one, and nothing outside our private little sphere mattered.

"Amir!" Sidig walked in dragging Maritsa, or more to the point, Maritsa was pulling him, trying to keep him from coming onto the terrace.

She was fussing up a storm. "Leave them be. It can wait."

"It cannot wait. He has to know."

"No, he doesn't. He just kissed her. He finally brings a woman home to meet me, and you keep interrupting."

Maritsa's English was fabulous. She was also obviously eavesdropping.

"It's about the boat," Sidig said.

"I don't care. At the rate he's going, I will never see children here at the house. Let him be, so he can get this right," Maritsa countered.

My mouth dropped open.

Amir raised his hand to ward off any further discussion. "What's going on?"

"Amir, we have a problem." He stopped in front of us. Maritsa had a smug look on her face, like she caused the problem.

"What happened?"

He turned and pointed at the sky. Off in the distance, dark clouds were rolling in, shots of lightning made a jagged path toward the earth. "A storm is coming. We will not be able to launch the boat for her return to the mainland."

Right on cue, a gust of wind blew in from the ocean. It knocked over the glasses on the table. They fell with a clink and dropped wine onto our unfinished meal. Maritsa shook her head and began to clear the table.

"Here, let me help you," I offered.

She waved me off. "You stay with him. Keep him smiling."

I know matchmaking 101 when I see it. Then it hit me, she thought I was Zahra. "Oh no, I am not who you think I am."

She stopped briefly and gave me a conspiratorial wink; the load of dishes teetered in her hand. "You are his fiancée. That is who you are." She pulled a pouch out of her pocket. "I used the bones in this pouch to ask Ola the goddess of the wind to bring a storm to keep you here. Now, work your magic on him." With that, she spun around and walked off.

I was completely thrown off guard.

What kind of crazy situation had I been dragged into?

Sidig waited until she was out of earshot. "We also have intel."

Amir snapped to attention; his entire demeanor changed. He was all business. "What is it?"

"Mustapha tracked us to this location."

Amir shook his head. "That's impossible."

"I said the same thing," Sidig replied.

Amir turned to look at me. "We have to get you inside until we find out what is going on."

Chapter 6

*A*mir

I ushered Angela to my room. She was a vision. A goddess. The braids were gone and, in their place light auburn curls cascaded around her shoulders. The beautiful orange and red dress Maritsa had given her looked like the sunset on a summer afternoon.

Our kiss filled a void lodged deep in my soul. I craved more. She was the lavender and jasmine balm I realized was missing from my life. It took all my strength to step away and secure the house when I preferred to stay there by her side.

Sidig had gone off to close his portion of the house. We had storm windows installed last year, and all of them had to be secured. "*Ahnjela*, wait here while I close the house down."

"Can I help?" she asked. Her voice felt like smooth water sliding over my skin. "No, I can handle it. Relax here, and I'll return soon."

The perimeter of the house and the boat dock were secured. Sidig's news of Mustapha tracking us was unsettling. I had time to make a few calls, and checked some leads, but no one had any useful information.

On my way to the guest room, I checked on Angela. She was a vision of beauty. I tried not to stare at how her dress buttoned beneath her breasts. They stood at attention and called my name. I blinked once, twice, then settled my eyes on her face, the one safe location for them to rest. I wanted to walk in and scoop her up but held myself back, thankful my loose shirt hid my raging hard-on. Or, at least I hoped it did.

She'd seen my desire for her earlier when I pulled her from the lagoon. At some point in this day, I should show some control. I cleared my throat before I spoke, "I came by to see if you need anything."

She hesitated a few seconds. "I'm fine. I was just about to turn in."

A gust of wind hit the patio doors making them rattle. I walked over to secure them tighter. When I turned around, she was standing by the bed. The light from the lamp glowed softly behind her, revealing her curves. I swallowed hard and walked to the door.

One more night. I could keep away from her tonight. If I said it enough times, it would be true. When the storm passed, I would send her home. We would go back to our lives. The thought of sending her away made me ill, but I knew it would have to be done for her safety. "Call me if you need me."

Two hours later the full force of the storm hit the island. I was still awake thinking of Angela's soft curves snuggled up against me and that sweet smile on her lips.

I was nodding off when I heard a crash coming from my room.

Angela screamed.

I was up and at the door in a second.

I rushed into the room to find Angela fighting with the doors. The latch had come loose, and the door was banging into the wall.

This was the sound I'd heard.

Rain pelted into the room. Angela was in the middle of it all soaking wet and trying to close the door herself. I ran to help her. We both slipped on the wet tile but finally got the door reseated and closed.

With the door tied down and the storm firmly left outside, I turned to see if she was okay. She was breathing heavily, soaking wet and looking like she had swum a fifty-meter race. I guided her over to the bed. "Are you alright?"

She nodded. "Yes." She plucked at her wet gown. It showed all her beautiful curves and full breasts. I grew hard at the thought of taking her nipple into my mouth. They were taut under the material. I chastised myself. *The lady must be cold standing here in these wet clothes.*

"Let me get you a towel," I said.

"Thanks, that would be wonderful." Water dripped down her legs. "I'm afraid I'm making a puddle on your floor."

"Don't worry about it." I retrieved a couple of towels and handed one to her.

She delicately wiped her face and drew the towel around her. "Do you think Maritsa has another gown I can borrow?"

I could not take my eyes off her lips. A low roar started in my ears, and all I could think about was tasting her. I circled my towel around her and pulled her to me capturing her lips. My tongue darted out and tangled with hers. She returned the kiss with equal passion. I was lost in her essence and goodness and did not deserve her but was too weak to push her away. Maybe if she told me to go, I would have the strength. Maybe if I told her I was a thief and a smuggler, she would kick me out. "I can't stop on my own. Please send me away," I pleaded.

I cradled her face in the palm of my hands. Those hazel-colored eyes drilled straight into my heart. She shifted her shoulder, and one side of the gown slipped off. I tried again. "*Ahnjela*, Habibi, I am not a nice man. I have done bad things."

Her voice was husky and low. "Have you done illegal things?"

I nodded with a whisper. "Yes."

"Have you killed anyone?"

I nodded again. "Yes."

"Do you love Zahra?" she whispered.

"No," I answered quickly." I could not imagine what she thought of me, engaged to a complete stranger.

She paused and put her forehead against mine. "Why did you agree to marry her?"

The reasons seemed petty now. In our world, we did it all the time. But, once Angela walked into my life, I could see the folly of my ways. I could have come up with a clever lie but only the truth would do for her. "For money and political gain."

With tears in her eyes, she pushed me away. I never wanted to be the reason for her tears. They crushed my heart and threatened to strangle me. "What about Zahra? That's not fair to her," she cried.

I hung my head. "I have no excuse."

"Would you treat me the same as Zahra?" she asked.

I understood her logic. If I would only consider marriage for profit and political gain to one woman, would I do it to another? How could I explain I would never do that to her? *Ever.*

In these few short hours, she had won my heart. I held my hand over my chest. "May my mother come and strike me dead if I ever hurt you."

I reached down and raised the gown strap over her shoulders. Staying here would lead us down a path we dared not go. She needed to go home and leave me and my twisted world behind. I turned to leave, but she stopped me. "Can you look in the drawer over there and see if Maritsa left me an extra gown."

There were no gowns, but I found one of my old, comfortable shirts in the drawer and returned to her side. She'd already kicked off the wet gown and had the towel wrapped around her. "Here you go."

"Thanks." Her smile produced a small dimple on her right cheek. "You're dripping wet. You might as well grab some dry clothes while you're in here."

I nodded and returned to get something dry. I was almost to the door when she asked one more question.

"What does habibi mean?"

I froze. The word had slipped out of my mouth as if it was always meant for her. I had never called any other woman, 'habibi'.

She stood there in the soft light, wrapped in a towel, her hair all around her shoulders in wet curls. My heart tripped. Watching her stole my breath away. I never imagined this accidental kidnapping could take me on such an emotional roller coaster.

I was in front of her before I knew it, kissing all her tears away. "It means 'my love'."

My wet clothes landed in a puddle beside her. The towel slipped from her shoulders and soon joined them. I picked her up and placed her in the middle of the bed. The storm raged outside, rattling the doors and windows. We were in our own warm cocoon, oblivious to it all.

I kissed and nibbled her ear, her neck and moved down to the bounty of her breasts. Hers were big, brown and beautiful. I slowly sucked one then the other carefully teasing them into hard peaks.

My next stop was the tight bud between her legs. She moaned when I stopped there, her voice a sonnet to my ears. I could listen to her cries of passion all night. One finger, then two slipped in while I worked her clit harder. She unraveled in my arms, her scream amplified by orgasmic bliss. I was on an adrenaline overload, and there was only one thing I could do to sate my burning desire.

I crawled back up and positioned myself above her. She bucked her hips attempting to take me in.

"Eager?" I asked.

"You're driving me out of my mind," she answered.

I kissed her, moving my tongue deep, at the same time I entered her. I wanted to take my time, worship her, caress her and watch her reaction. Learn what drives her desires. But, my control evaporated with our first kiss. She was fine wine that needed to be sipped and savored. Our combined drive for pleasure negated my overriding desire to go slow and explore.

She gasped as I sank into her hot core. I pulled out and entered again, each time going deeper and lingering longer. Her eyes glazed over; her cries of pleasure husky and passionate. This drove me wild, but I kept a steady pace. I loved watching her react to our connection. She moved her hips, bucking into me with increasing speed.

"I think you want me to go a little faster."

She uttered one word, "Yes."

I wanted to take my time, and maintain my pace, enjoying the tight slide as she wrapped me in her velvet sheath and moved her hips in a circular motion. Yeah, I could do this all night. She was my exotic flower and only tender care would do for her. But, my sweet Angela had other plans that demanded deep, intense passion that was impossible for me to deny.

Her nails dug into my back making me wild. Then she raised her hand and smacked my rear end.

"Faster," she ordered.

What control I had evaporated. The woman sent me soaring to the sky, and I moved faster and harder, she rose to meet me stroke for stroke. She wrapped her legs around mine; we were both out of our minds reaching for that perfect place to launch our souls to the sky.

"*Ahnjela,* let go, and I will catch you."

She arched her back and stilled, the tension unwound, electric fire began at the base of my spine and wound itself around my cock until our world shattered apart.

I kissed her. "*Ahnjela*, I want this night to last forever."

She caressed my face and curled up beside me. "We can try."

Chapter 7

Angela

He. Was. Crack.

And, I was the addict riding high on the white-hot train to heaven. I'd never had such an emotional response to any man. Amir touched a nerve in me, one that drove deep and lodged in my heart. His kisses branded me wherever they landed, lips, throat, nipples all the secret spaces and places.

We were wild, loud, unrepentant in our desires of the flesh. He fulfilled my fantasies of romantic sex in some exotic, remote hideaway. The world, and its demands, no longer existed. There was no one to hear or judge us.

We fell into a deep slumber, nestled in each other's arms. I'd always wondered what it would be like to snuggle against a hard, male body who was insatiable for more. Amir did not disappoint.

I awoke to his intense gaze. He studied me like I was a new found work of art. Cherished. Desired. I stretched, working out kinks from my sore but happy muscles.

"Don't move," his voice a rumbled whisper. "I want to look at you, learn every inch of you."

I'd never been the subject of absolute devotion before. I considered myself average, nothing to get excited about. But, the intensity in his eyes as they roved over every inch of my skin was laser focused. Precise. He didn't want to miss a thing.

This was a unique experience for me. Curiosity overrode my instinct to remain quiet and observe. The question sprang from my mouth of its own volition. "What's so fascinating?"

His lips descended toward my hip, his hand stroked my thigh. "You're an exotic work of art." Electric ropes of fire radiated from his contact with my skin. I arched into the sensation.

"I must worship you." He moved higher. My skin pebbled in anticipation. He lowered his lips in a slow measured glide. His tongue darted out, tasting, probing making my breath escaped in short gasps.

"You fascinate me." His hand ran along my waist, up my rib cage holding me still for his intense inspection. He took his time leaving hot, steam filled kisses in his wake.

I fascinate him? I'm exotic?

I've never seen this reaction in a man. Ever. Yet, he meant every word. He reached my breasts, cupped each one with his hands. Feeling their weight and measure. By now, little tremors ran through me, moisture leaked between my thighs. His exploration took me to new levels of sensual overload.

His mouth lavished careful attention to each nipple. His tongue swirled, his teeth tugged, nipped. He blew on each tip. Kissed them. Cherished them. A mewling noise escaped my lips. He chuckled, sending vibrations rocketing through my system. Any more input to my overloaded sensual receptors and combustion was a dangerous possibility.

"I've wanted to do this from the moment I pulled you from the lagoon, soaking wet, your dress transparent." He blew hot air over the peaks and returned to his devotion.

I believed him to the core of my soul. His was a face of a zealot waiting to worship at the temple. Wanting, no, needing to touch and feel my peaks and valleys. He rose a few more inches and found my neck. A kiss, a swirl of the tongue, a nip of his teeth. He drove me insane with his intense, raw desire.

My lips were next on his pilgrimage. He feasted in delight. Our tongues tangled in a duet of passion and fire.

His hips shifted and spread my legs wide. He'd arrived at the gates of the temple. I was more than ready to receive, moisture bathed my thighs and coated my skin.

His breath, heavy with need pushed new energy into me. "Open your eyes, *Ahnjela.*"

I'd closed them while writhing under his careful ministrations, unable to stop moving, desperate for more. His eyes where two dark orbs of heat and desire. I focused on him, my gaze locked with his. "I want us to watch each other as we ride the stairway to Heaven."

My breath caught, his declaration sent flash of need straight through me. He entered me in a slow, sensual glide to nirvana. Briefly, I tightened from the bite of his passage; my muscles constricted, then relaxed, as intense pleasure blossomed in my core. He was steel wrapped in silk. The perfect combination. My lids fluttered as my head tilted and I arched my back for deeper penetration.

"Stay focused, habibi."

My eyes snapped open on his command. "That's right... Feel me as I feel you." His voice caught. "You're exquisite."

I moved, undulating, urging him to go faster. Harder. Hotter.

He grasped my hands, sliding them above my head, stretching me out, forcing me tighter against his hard length. "Oh, *Ahnjela*, I'm going to cherish you and make you feel...ravished, loved."

My heart fluttered, a tremor raced through my core. I panted in anticipation.

His grin was wicked, sinful. "Your body is tuned to mine. I feel the tension thrumming through your veins. Be patient; this will take some time."

Amir's hot gaze drilled straight through me. We were locked in a sensual ballet, all movement and emotion. Our focus never wavered or wandered from each other as he played me like a string quartet.

He drew out each stroke, taking my breath away, making my head spin from extreme pleasure. I moved with him in and out as the symphony of our bodies played a sweet melody.

He was masterful, in his performance, changing his rhythm when my cries of pleasure became soft or quickened with frantic puffs of my breath. If my eyes closed from intense pleasure, he'd slow his tempo and wait patiently for them to open. He wanted my attention on us and our combined pleasure.

Amir's pace quickened, as we reached for that final note, the one that would take us to nirvana. His stroke drove deep and together we exploded into bliss screaming each other's names.

The patio doors flew open with a loud bang; rain blew in pebbling the bed and our bodies with its fury. We watched each other come apart and splinter into pieces as the storm raged around us, peppering us with its fury.

"*Ahnjela*," he said my name with a reverence I never thought I would hear from a man. It echoed up the walls and swirled away entwined in my gasps of pleasure.

I felt loved, desired…treasured. He took care of me in ways I found hard to describe. It was like he knew, on a deep and intimate level, what both sides of my personality needed to feel and hear. He accepted the rougher, DC Angela *and* the calm, rational Angela with equal passion. They were two pieces of the Angela puzzle no one had been able to figure out. Instinctively, he knew what to do to please them both and celebrated them in their complicated glory.

With a smile on my face, I nuzzled into him and threw my arm over his broad chest. DC hummed a happy tune while rational Angela purred its harmony. We were relaxed, content, yet amazed that Amir figured it out and was drawn to our flame.

Chapter 8

A mir

It was early morning. The storm had died down; I held her close, caressing her in slow, easy, strokes. She put a smile on my face nothing could take away. Her intelligence, passion, and exotic beauty challenged and intrigued me like no other. I could hold her all morning, lulled by the cadence of her breathing and the gentle breeze flowing in from the patio.

Several minutes later, I heard a strange sound.

Beep, pause, beep beep.

It was unfamiliar to me; all my alarms were set with music not beeps. I sat up abruptly and looked around the room. On the dresser, an old fashion clock with minute and hour hands was dark. The fluorescent arms were a source of light when I woke before the sun came up. Their absence was unusual. The rest of the room was shrouded in deep shadows. Outside, the small light on the patio was off.

Damn. The power went out.

Our sole source of illumination was the rising sun; its rays peaked over the horizon casting a warm glow on the glistening tiles of the patio. The doors hung open at odd angles, their hinges torn and mangled. Inside, the floor was slick from the rainwater and reflected a watery image of the swaying palm trees. A standing lamp had toppled over. The furniture and rugs were soaked. One panel of the curtain hung half torn and limp on the rod. The other was a sodden mess on the floor. The doors had blown open, causing all this damage—and I hadn't noticed. Was I that far gone with Angela?

Yes.

Soft curls framed her face, long lashes fanned over smooth, dark chocolate cheeks. Her lips were so full and sweet that every cell in my body said, kiss them, make them yours again. I could watch her for a lifetime, yet had to admit, if only to myself…

I could not give her up.

Even worse, what would I do when she had to leave?

Beep, pause, beep beep.

There it was again. I decided to go find the damned thing. But first, I gave into temptation and captured Angela's lips with mine. She mumbled and threw her arms around me for a deeper kiss.

Oh, the passion in this woman had no bounds.

I paused a moment to savor the bounty of her lips, then disentangled her arms, got up and followed the sound to the bathroom.

A dish full of beads from her hair sat on the counter.

Beep, pause, beep beep.

The last two beeps came faster than before.

Is it under the cabinet?

A flashlight was kept in the drawer in case of a blackout. I retrieved it and got down on the floor, rolled over and pointed the light under the cabinet.

What the hell could it possibly be?

The sound was louder now, the pitch higher, more focused. With my hand, I patted around until it grazed a small round smooth object. I sat up and shined the light. It was one of the beads from her braids; only this one blinked on and off. I got up and examined it closer. Embedded on the side was a tiny transmitter.

Sidig's words flowed through my mind. *We have intel; Mustapha is mounting a raid against us.*

I could not figure out how Mustapha would be able to find us. Now, I knew. He planted this transmitter in her hair. That's why he was so eager to agree to a wire transfer.

He wanted me to pick her up as soon as possible.

If she were sick, I would have to bring her home to keep it quiet. That's why he drugged her.

Shit, they could be here already.

"*Ahnjela!*" I ran to the bed and gathered her up. "We have to get dressed and go." I grabbed my phone and called Sidig. "Get Maritsa and the rest of the staff out of here. I found a transmitter. Mustapha is coming."

Angela heard me. "What?"

"He planted a transmitter in your hair." I showed her the bead as I pulled her up.

"Is that one of my beads?" She looked confused, yet adorable, with the bed sheets pulled up around her. The curls of her hair were tighter and rose from her head in every direction. She was ravishing and well loved. I did that to her. Those lips, sweet nectar from a jasmine tree, drew me in. I wanted to kiss her, take the sheet from around her, run my hands over her body, through her hair. I was under her hypnotic spell, and she did not even know she was doing it to me.

Beep, pause, beep, beep, beep.

The bead vibrated and gave off an extra beep, the sound shrill and incessant in the still of the dark room. It must have scared the daylights out of her. She yelped and jumped, knocking the bead out of my grasp. It bounced and rolled down the valleys of the rumpled folds in the sheet.

My mind snapped back to the more pressing issue at hand. We had to get out. I patted the bed down, found the bead, ran to the patio and threw it as hard as I could as a way to confuse the trackers into thinking we were somewhere else. Angela stood by the bed wrapped in a sheet. I would have to take the time later to figure out how one look at her could take my focus away so completely. But, for now, getting out of here was more urgent than ever. The third beep meant they were closer.

I scooped clothes out of my drawer and gave them to her. "Yes, that is your bead. Put these on; we must leave now."

She pulled on my pants and shirt looking sexy as hell. *Damn.* I tore my gaze away and grabbed a belt. "This should keep the pants up."

I finished dressing, and was putting my shoes on, when I heard the low whistle. I grabbed Angela and pulled her into the bathroom just before the bedroom exploded.

The force of the explosion sent us sprawling deeper into the far corner of the bathroom. Smoke billowed around, flames licked at the edges of the doorframe. I pulled her closer to me, scanning the wreckage for an escape route. To my right, the room was an impassible mess. To my left, a waft of fresh air cleared the smoke enough for me to see a small hole in the wall of the bathroom. That would have to be our way out.

We both coughed. The smoke made it nearly impossible to breathe. "This way," I croaked and propelled Angela toward the hole. A column of flames burst through the bedroom door. Water flooded in from a broken pipe. I push Angela through, and I sloshed out behind her. Once outside the air cleared, but we were still coughing the last of the smoke out of our lungs. Shouts came from the front of the house. We could not go in that direction. I turned and pointed toward the towering grove of vanilla trees. It had been in our family for generations and fanned out behind the house for miles. Sidig and I had a prearranged meeting place, in case of emergencies, located on the far side of the jungle.

A small clearing separated the house and the vanilla grove. It was large enough to expose us as we dashed across. I gripped Angela's hand tighter, sent up a silent prayer that we would not be seen and ran.

A shout echoed through the air as we reached the edge of the grove. Two more steps and we were in the trees, running headlong into outstretched branches, leaves and vines. Guns roared to life, bullets zinged and ricocheted to our right, impacting the tree with a soggy thud. "Keep your head down," I yelled and pushed her forward, making sure I was between her and the unknown sniper as more bullets hit the trees uncomfortably close to our heads.

We ran for almost ten minutes, our footsteps thankfully muted by the dense underbrush. Above, in the canopy, morning sunlight floated down, a bright, shining promise for a hot and humid day. The jungle floor was a slippery mass of wet foliage that threatened our footing every step of the way. Insect noise and animal chatter followed in our wake as we crashed through the trees.

"Stop... I have to take a break," Angela said between short gasps of breath. Her chest heaved pulling in every ounce of air possible.

I looked back. There was no sign of pursuit. "Okay, one minute. We're almost to our ride out of here."

She glanced around. Trees and dense underbrush surrounded us. I understood her confusion; neither cars nor motor scooters could get through this stuff. "Let me show you."

Around a fallen log and two more massive vanilla trees lay my climbing apparatus. It was wet and battered from the storm but still serviceable. "This is our ride. You go first."

"Where?"

I pointed up.

Angela's faced was a mask of horror. She backed away, her eyes wide as saucers.

Chapter 9

Angela

"Oh, hell no!"

I spun on my heels looking for an escape. A green wall of vegetation rose up in front of me. Trees, one hundred feet tall, crowded the space, each vying for the soil, sunshine and rain. The air was closed in, humid and thick with the rich scent of wood and vanilla. Monkeys chittered away in the limbs of the trees. Deep growls of predators lurked in the shadows. A jungle surrounded me with no way out. Desperately, my mind tried to ignore the nagging, cloying feeling of being boxed in and claustrophobic. My first instinct was to press the panic button, but this would not be a good idea. Instead, I breathed in deeply and exhaled. Amir placed his hands on my shoulders, in an attempt to comfort me.

"Ahnjela, it's okay. I'll talk you through it."

He wants me to climb a tree. My God.

Up into the canopy, sunlight filtered through thick leaves and vines. It sparkled through the drops of dew and rain that still clung to them. The thought of going up there shook me to the core.

"*Ahnjela*, what is the problem?"

"I'm afraid of heights." A slow tremble worked its way through my left side. "Nope, not gonna go up there. I've been kidnapped, drugged, romanced, blown up and dragged through a jungle. I'm done. No way are you getting me up a tree."

"You took a plane to get here. That goes much higher than a tree."

"I didn't look out the window," I screamed.

A tremor ran through my entire body, my pulse raced. At least on the plane, I'd had a full glass of wine in my system, a mask to cover my eyes and an iPod full of jazz music. Without proper medicinal intervention, he was demanding I do an impossible task.

We walked, or rather, we ran here, surely we could run out. I searched for an escape route, but there was no obvious path; a wall of green vegetation stood before us. Solid. Impenetrable. My chest heaved, and I began to hyperventilate.

"*Ahnjela*, look at me." Amir moved to stand in front of me and bent a little, so his eyes were level with mine. "Habibi, you can do this. I set up a system of ziplines to make it easier to pollinate then harvest the vanilla. It will also allow us to get quite a distance ahead of them."

"Pollinate? Harvest?" I heard him. It made sense. BUT, the thought of so much air under my feet, kept me firmly rooted to the ground. "Shoot me now."

He put his forehead to mine, a deep chuckle rumbled through his chest. "No, I'm not going to shoot you."

His lips grazed mine, and the quick kiss turned into a sensual lip-smacking, torch burning full-on-sizzled kiss. My head swam.

Far off in the distance was the sound of twigs breaking. "The men are getting close. We've got to climb, now."

I breathed so hard it hurt. He was right, but my feet remained stuck to the ground. "What's the worse they would do to us?"

He strode toward the tree dragging me with him. "Mustapha is angry with me. If he doesn't kill you outright, then he will rape you and sell you into slavery."

I froze, my voice caught in my throat. This shit just took a left turn toward hell. What was he saying to me? "Amir, slavery doesn't exist."

"Yes, it does, and I'm trying to keep you out of it." He picked me up and carried me to the edge of a tree. His cinnamon and musk scent made me want to pant. His strength was intoxicating. He held me like a China doll.

"I must get you out of here and back to safety." He reached up, the muscles in his chest bunched and corded. His hand returned holding rigging for the climb. This was happening.

Someone shouted, the rasp of his voice echoed between the trees.

Amir's hands were a blur. "They're here; we have to go."

The harness was on me and secured before I could protest more. He grabbed a rope and pulled. "Hang on."

The whole rigging jerked, and my body rose. I grabbed onto the rope like it was my golden lifeline, and it was. Then it occurred to me, I didn't know what to do at the top. "Amir, how do I get out of this once I'm up there?"

"There will be a small platform. Step onto it, unhook from this line, and then give it a tug. Go around the tree and find the handle that is attached to the zipline. Clip yourself to that."

He tugged on the rope, the harness lifted me toward the branches above. Leaves, flowers and vines slid by. I squealed, then closed my eyes. Finally, the ride stopped, and I peeked.

The jungle had changed from deep shadows and muted green foliage to bright light, and tropical beauty. Down on the ground my chest was heavy, breathing labored, the air felt like you could cut it with a knife. At the top, the air was crisp and cool, the weight lifted off my lungs. But, what struck me the most was the beauty spread out before me. The canopy was rich, green and full of colorful flowers and life. Insects buzzed, birds flew in and out and monkeys dashed from limb to limb. I exhaled, having forgotten to breathe on the way up. "Wow." Seemed like such a weak word to describe the view.

Far below, Amir gave the line a hard tug. That meant he needed help.

Dear Lord, what did he tell me to do? Find the platform.

There was nothing around that remotely resembling a platform. I scanned the tree a second time. On the left side of the tree, were some wooden boards.

That can't be it.

The wood splintered when my toe touched the edge. It fell away smacking leaves and branches in its wake.

My God, there's so much air beneath me.

I clutched the rope in a death grip, praying my sweating palms maintained their hold.

Buried between leaves and pale yellow flowers was another weathered wooden board.

It's the rest of the platform.

I dragged in two deep breaths and swayed my body back and forth. On the third swing my foot landed. The board held firm. I scrambled, scraping my shin in the process, but managed to glue myself like a wood nymph onto what was left of the boards.

I was out of breath, in a panic and shook like the leaves surrounding me. Half of the platform had blown away in the storm. Somehow, I'd found the remaining portion of it. My arm circled a large branch for safety, just in case the pitiful section of wood beneath me decided to give way.

This is freaking me out. I'm not made for swinging through trees!

Amir shouted and tugged the line again. I released myself and made my way to the other side. The boards ran around the circumference of the tree. Zipline bars and hooks to connect my harness were dangling from a branch.

He wanted me to put my faith in this thing?

The set of boards holding me were bedraggled and half knocked away. How on earth could he think the zipline was good?

With a *whoosh,* Amir appeared near me. He swung once and was on the boards. They wobbled but held his weight. "That wasn't bad."

"Not bad? Do you see the state of this thing?" My voice cracked.

Before he could answer, shouts echoed from below. Gunshots erupted, and bullets whipped through the trees. "Get down," Amir ordered, covering me with his body.

The guns stopped, and all was eerily quiet. Someone tugged on the cord holding Amir. He lost his balance and almost fell into the void below before I grabbed his waist and pulled him back onto the relative safety of the platform. With a flip of his wrist, he released himself from the rope, it slithered out of view thwacking leaves in its wake.

"Thanks for catching me."

He led me around the tree and smoothly hooked me to the zipline. "Keep your knees to your chest as you go."

I shook, my voice quivered. "But, what about the far side? Is it damaged? Will it hold our weight? Is the platform still there?"

"Honestly, I don't know. But, there is one thing I do know—"

I finished his thought. "We can't stay here."

He nodded, rubbed my back and nudged me toward the edge. "Try not to make a sound. He can't track us, if he doesn't know which way we're headed."

Out over the canopy, a sea of green undulated like a lumpy carpet. The line disappeared between massive trees, its end obscured and hidden in shadow. More gunfire whipped through the leaves. I said a prayer. He pushed me, and I stepped out into the air.

Chapter 10

*A*mir

*A*ngela screamed the whole way across. She started with, "*Help me, Jeeeesuuuus.*" and ended with "*Awww, helllll.*"

Her voice echoed over the entire canopy. The top of the trees shook as she passed disturbing a flock of turacos. Their blue and red plumage beat the air in a fury of wings and feathers. They called to each other in a cacophony of tweets and caws. If Mustapha did not know which way we were heading, he did now.

I settled my hook on the line and leaped. My trajectory sent me through the middle of the flock. I tucked myself in tighter as flapping wings and bird beaks collided with my body. Their screams of outrage rang in my ears. Thankfully, my speed of travel quickly zipped me beyond their fury and out into clear air. The jungle canopy whipped by, its green foliage a blur of dappled sunlight, flowers and leaves. A massive tree loomed before me. In its shadows, Angela dangled from the harness desperately grasping a branch, her face a mask of fear. The platform sat to the right, damaged by the storm and completely out of her reach.

"*Ahnjela*, look out. I'm right behind you."

Instinctively, I pulled my legs up to slow down and stop behind her. I gathered her in my arms. She shook, refusing to release the branch, her breath came out in hard puffs. "Half of the platform," she gulped in air. "Is gone."

She was sandwiched between me and the rough wood of the tree. Her soft curves melted into me, bringing back images of last night. I cleared my throat. "We're okay," I reassured her.

"That's what you say." She waved at a section of the board nestled against a stout limb. "It's too far."

"Listen, together we're going to swing close enough to jump." I counted to three and used my feet to push. We swung out, angling toward the remaining section of the platform. She bent her knees and pushed off with me the second swing. By the third, we'd managed to get close enough to jump onto the board. It shook but held our combined weight.

The line for the next platform was a few paces around the tree. "We must hook ourselves up there."

She glared at me; the fire in her eyes could have burned through wood. "You want me to swing on another one of these?"

I helped her higher up onto the boards. "We have to glide down this one, then one more. The last one will be over the river."

She inhaled. "Okaaay, I'll be fine." She bunched up her fists. "No, I won't. I will not be fine," she yelled.

"*Ahnjela*, look. The lines and the platforms should be in better condition. They are farther away from the house, and it looked like the worst of the storm hit near the house."

She wagged her finger at me. "Right, but if I die, I am coming back to haunt you."

She allowed me to hook her up to the line. We zipped over to the next tree one thousand yards away. Mercifully the platform was in much better shape than the last two.

One more slide and we had arrived at the river crossing. The vanilla grove was behind us, and we were deep in the jungle. The river, usually placid and slow, was flooded to the brim, the water turbulent and murky. I tugged on the line and felt its taut twang in my fist. "It looks good, let's go."

She scanned the area resigned to our course of action. "Is this the last one?"

"Yes." I drew her closer to me than necessary, my hands on her waist to steady her. The gesture was natural, like we'd been together for years.

She noticed the way I held her and shifted toward me. "Amir, I…" She stopped unsure of what to say. "About last night…I…"

The waters raged below us as turbulent as our thoughts and hearts. *About last night, indeed.*

I caressed her cheek. "I will treasure the memory of last night for the rest of my life."

Her eyes fluttered, tears formed. She put her forehead against my chest. "Don't do this to me."

I rubbed her back. "Do what?"

"You make me feel special. Like I am the queen of the world."

"You are my queen."

She lifted her head. "Then reality clicks in and..." She stopped, her lips quivered. She shook her head and looked out over the river; her face as troubled as the rushing water below.

I finished the thought for her. "Reality clicks in, and I push you out of a tree?"

She sniffed, wiped her eyes and straightened up. "Something like that." She pointed. "I guess I better get started across."

I tightened her harness and kissed her. It was impossible not to kiss her. She was sweet sugar spun of golden sunshine. Oh God, I was making up poetry about her. I needed to stop and be realistic. She was right; reality would eventually kick in, it always does. I would have to send her home, and I was not sure if I was strong enough to do so when the time came.

I moved out of her way, so she could get going. This last time, however, her eyes were open, her back straight, her face set and determined. A high-pitched squeal issued from her throat as she stepped off into the void. The oddest thing happened halfway across; she began to laugh. Her laughter followed her down the line.

I crossed over a few minutes later and met her on the platform. It was solid, unscathed by the storm. "You seemed to enjoy the last half of that."

She did a small victory dance. "Did you see me? It was great!"

"Absolutely. What changed?"

She shrugged. "I decided to embrace my fear. What's the worst that could happen?"

I unhooked her from the line. "You could die and come back to haunt me?"

She moved close, clouding my senses with her sweet smell of lavender and jasmine. "Or, I live, and we have a good long talk about last night."

I was always up for a good conversation, but first, I had to get her down out of this tree. I had a stash on the platform of gloves and extra rope; everything was in place as I'd left it. I handed them to her and hooked her up for the ride down to the ground. "I can't wait for our lively discussion. But first…I have to push you out of yet another tree."

She gave me a wicked grin, and after some quick instructions, rode down to the ground.

I followed and met her at the bottom. The ground was dry, the air thick and humid. Trees were intact and the trail was clear, this portion of the jungle was spared the storm's wrath. I pointed off to the left. "We go this way. We're about a mile from my jungle retreat."

Angela raised an eyebrow. "Retreat?"

"You'll see. We should be safe for a few hours. Once we've rested, we'll take the jeep I've stashed there and drive to the port. It'll take about two hours…if the road is clear."

The hike was challenging; each step took more energy than the last. Leaves and twigs snapped beneath our feet; the path was uneven and partially covered. We scrambled under low hanging limbs and pushed through dense brush. Without a machete, it was impossible to cut through the thicker patches of foliage and vines. I pulled them away to let Angela pass, and dashed pass them, before they whipped back into place.

Angela was winded and sweaty but did not complain, even though she clearly did not like her proximity to the insect life that flourished on the jungle floor. She watched me closely and mimicked my movement. Soon her steps were more economic, taking less energy. Her breathing leveled out, and we were able to pick up speed. We hiked through the jungle for an hour and a half before the hut came into view. "*Ahnjela,* we're here."

It was a solid construction of hardwood and cement. Four squat walls held a slanted roof made of tin. I built it in the middle of a group of date palm trees and dense bushes rendering it nearly invisible to a casual glance. We waited a few yards back; everything appeared in order. The outside of the hut showed no signs of habitation or disturbance.

We worked our way over to the door. It swung open with a nudge from my hand. My shoulders tensed; I'd left the place securely locked. There was no way Mustapha could have gotten ahead of us much less knew our destination but, after the attack, I took nothing for granted. Cautiously, I leaned inside. It was dark, the air musty and still. Exactly how I'd expected to find it, except for the shadowed figure, which stood in the far corner with a gun pointed directly at my heart. The slow click of its hammer made my blood run cold.

Chapter 11

*A*ngela

I heard the click of the gun and froze. Amir blocked my view of the interior, preventing me from seeing inside. He made a whistling sound of tweets, two short, two long and two short again. A man grabbed him and pulled him in. This was an attack. Someone knew about this place and was in there waiting for us.

Enough was enough! I had just spent a harrowing morning swinging through the trees like Jane of the Jungle after surviving an attempt on my life. I hiked through an insect-infested jungle and in this heat and humidity, sweat every ounce of water my body possessed. My mind snapped; DC Angela said, *Jump them.*

I ran in screaming and leaped onto both men, knocking them to the floor. We fell in a jumble of legs, feet and arms.

"*Ahnjela,*" Amir shouted from the bottom of the pile.

I rolled off them and got up with my fists out front and ready to fight. I was done being the victim.

Amir untangled himself from the man who got up and pulled the curtain aside. Light filtered into the room and I could see it was…

"Sidig?"

Amir waived his hand toward him. "Yes, it is. He recognized my whistle."

Sidig stared at me like he could not believe I'd just jumped him. He rubbed his back and gave me a half smile. "It is good to see you…I think."

"Sorry, I didn't know it was you," I said as I peered around the space.

The hut had a sink, a chair placed beside a metal chest and a small camping grill in one corner. A curtain was drawn across the room, dividing the space in two. I assumed there was a bed on the other side. This was a basic one-room cabin, quite serviceable in a pinch. We were in a pinch if ever I saw one.

Something or rather someone was missing. "Where is Maritsa?" I asked.

Sidig stepped over to the curtain and pulled it aside. "I'm glad you two made it here. I wasn't going to wait any longer. She was hit by shrapnel; she needs to get to a doctor. I was about to take the Jeep and drive her there."

"Bibi." Amir threw the curtain aside, rushing to the bed. Her inert form was ashen and still.

I shoved my way around Amir to get a better look. "What does Bibi mean?" I asked while I began to work on her.

"It means grandmother." His eyes were brimming.

85

I had no idea she was his grandmother. Even though I probably should have guessed from the way she meddled in his romantic affairs. I checked her pulse. It was weak. I removed the blanket Sidig had placed around her. Blood pooled from her side. My medical training, along with practical Angela, kicked in. "Do you have a med kit in this cabin?"

"Yes, I'll get it," Amir replied. He got up and crossed to the other side of the room and opened the chest.

Sidig leaned over me. "What are you doing?"

"Trying to save her life. We can't move her in this condition. Let me see if I can stabilize her."

"I don't understand. How can you help her?"

Amir returned with the kit. "She's a doctor."

There was pride in his voice. I glanced his way and saw a big grin on his face.

He was proud of me.

Wow, no man, other than my father, had ever been proud of me.

Sidig apparently had never heard of female doctors and wanted to argue. "That's not possible."

Amir put his hand up, halting any further protest. "She *is* a doctor; let her work."

By now, I had a good look at Maritsa's injury. It was a two-inch gash on her hip that needed cleaning, sutures and a bandage. The emergency kit had antibacterial ointment, gauze and oddly enough, super glue. There was no suture material in the kit, but I could make do with the glue. This was going to hurt though. "Do you have anything for pain?"

Amir nodded. "Yes."

"Get it. She's going to need it when I'm finish."

Once I began to work on her, the pain woke her up. I expected her to respond the same as Sidig upon hearing the news I was a doctor. Instead, she grinned from ear to ear. "I knew you were special. My grandson found a doctor…" She writhed in pain.

"Amir, give her the pain pills. Maritsa, you must chew them so they dissolve faster and get into your system quicker," I said to her.

She patted my hand. "Don't worry about me."

I cleaned the area, pulled the two parts together and glued them shut. Super glue works wonders for tacking wounds together.

Sidig cringed. "Are you sure she's a doctor? She just super glued Bibi."

Maritsa chuckled then winced in pain. "Hush, Sidig; she can glue me if she wishes… I'm so happy I found her before I die."

"Bibi, don't talk that way. You're not going to die," Amir hissed.

She grabbed his hand. "I promised your mother I would find you a good and smart wife. Then one day she lands in our lap."

She was animated and moved around.

"Maritsa, you have to stay still if this is going to hold. I don't have anything to suture you with, so this will have to do." She needed several stitches, and all I had was the glue. I tried to ignore what she was saying to

87

Amir as I finished tacking her skin together. She spoke in English, I was sure for my benefit.

Amir shook his head. "Quiet, Bibi; let her finish."

"Of course, Grandson. I am so happy now, I could fly. I'd given up hope, but here she is. She is smart, beautiful, and she keeps you happy in bed. Ouch!"

My hand slipped accidentally pulling her skin tighter. She must have been listening at the door last night. "Sorry."

She chuckled. "No need to apologize, Daughter. You two made more noise than the storm."

Sidig coughed and turned away, his shoulders shaking.

Oh God in heaven, let me please crawl into the wall and hide.

I finished with the glue; blood still seeped in one area. As long as she moved slowly, it would hold until we got her to town. I looked her straight in the eye. "I'm done now. I'll wrap it up, but I need you to be careful."

"Amir, is there a place for me to wash my hands before I put on the bandage?"

To his credit, he was unruffled. "The sink is functional this time of year."

"What do you mean?"

"It only works during the raining season and is off during the dry season." He followed me over to the sink. "I must apologize for my grandmother. She is concerned I have not started a family."

"Amir, I'm so embarrassed right now. I thought everyone was asleep last night."

"Sweetheart, it's okay—"

"Don't you, 'sweetheart me'," I protested.

Rational Angela was riding me hard. Admonishing me and listing a whole litany of my sins. The least of which was to spread my legs and let his hot body slide right in. I hiccupped as those images played in front of my mind's eye. "No, it's not okay. We should have had some control." I held up my index finger and thumb. "Some small amount of control."

He placed his hands on my hip, pulled me closer and wrapped his arms around my shoulders with a bone-searing hug.

Why did it feel so right and good?

"*Ahnjela*, habibi, we will figure it out," he whispered in my ear.

"Will we?" My voice caught. When he was this close, all I could hear was our hearts beating as one. The combination of his hot body and those muscles snuggled up against me, made my brain turn to mush.

Sidig cleared his throat. "Ah-hmm."

I pulled away. There was a towel on a hook. I stepped over to dry my hands and clear my thoughts.

I. Was. In. Trouble.

No man ever affected me this way. Amir was intelligent, mysterious and fine as hell. Exactly my type. I wanted him, knowing he was engaged, and I was leaving to collect my cousin and get on the next thing smoking for the good old U.S. of A.

I made the mistake of glancing at his eyes. They were hooded, dramatic, dark and oh, so sexy. All my determined plans evaporated like the jungle mist in the morning sun.

Yeah, I was in big, big trouble.

He ran the pads of his fingers over my cheek. They created a trail of liquid heat and smoke down the side of my face and continued straight through to my fluttering heart. Next stop was carnal desire and my eyes dropped to his groin then flicked back to his.

Amir gave me a crooked smile like he knew what I was thinking. "It's time I go check on the Jeep." He sauntered out the door.

Damn, I was busted again.

Sidig stood by the bed with his arms crossed and a lopsided grin on his face. He nodded toward the bandaging he'd set out. I was not sure of what to say and finally decided to say nothing at all. Any words spoken would make matters worse. He wasn't blind, and apparently, he knew what we did last night too.

I finished wrapping her wound and helped her to stand. "Do you think you can walk?

She took a step and nodded. "Don't worry about me. You stay with him. He needs you."

What could I do? I was raised to mind and respect my elders. She was no different. But then, who was I kidding? All my compasses pointed toward Amir. I left the cabin and found him walking back from the woods. "The Jeep is ready."

We needed to talk and get a few things straight about last night. I had to figure out if we were a one-night stand or would there be more. He seemed to be so sincere, but he had a fiancée, and plans that did not include me. "Amir—"

"*Ahnjela*, I have to send you away for your protection, and it's killing me."

"What are you saying?"

He shifted from one foot to the other. "I want you to stay here...with me...and be in my life."

Chapter 12

*A*mir

The words left my mouth of their own volition. She was stunned, and I am not sure I blamed her. I wanted to tell her the truth about my business and why Mustapha was after us. More importantly, I wanted to tell her how I felt.

"Amir, my life is a world away and so different from yours. I couldn't stay here worrying about who is going to kidnap me or blow me up. I need to think about...everything," She paused. "Let's concentrate on getting Maritsa to a clinic. Where is the Jeep?"

I pointed toward the road. "It's on the other side of the trees."

Sidig appeared at the door holding Maritsa in his arms. He carried her to the Jeep with Angela and myself following in his wake. I had no choice but to continue my confession later when we got to the port. My grandmother was a handful, and this was one conversation I definitely did not want to have with her around.

The ride to the capital, Stone Town, was hot and bumpy. The storm had washed the road away in a lot of places. We passed people on foot and small cars brimming with families. Traffic was snarled and our progress slow. The jungle eventually gave way to cultivated fields and houses began to dot the landscape as we neared our destination.

We arrived four hours later to the cool welcome of the ocean breezes. It was still hot and humid, but the air was lighter and full of the smells from the spice market, which dominated the center of the city. Stone town was much smaller and less crowded than Dar es Salaam; it would make evading detection by Mustapha's people harder. I was on my guard as soon as we reached the outer city limits.

We took Maritsa to a clinic where a doctor saw her and sutured her wound. She was given a tetanus shot, and her bandages were replaced. He was impressed with Angela's quick thinking on using the super glue. I was about to brag about her when Sidig elbowed me. He was right, she was supposed to be Zahra, the chief's daughter. We could not risk exposing her identity. I had to let him think I had taken care of the wound.

I sent Sidig to the port to get the tickets for their passage to Dar es Salaam. Maritsa correctly pointed out that Angela could not walk around in a man's pants and top. We went to the other side of the spice market where several rows of shops were dedicated to clothes, jewelry and household items.

Merchants stood in front of their stalls calling out to prospective customers angling to entice them in and buy their wares. Tanzanian music blared from every booth. Seabirds flew overhead, calling out to one another, adding to the hum and vibe of the market.

Through it all, Angela's eyes were everywhere as if trying to look at everything at once. She seemed oblivious to the stares she was getting because she wore men's clothes.

I steered us to a shop loaded to the brim with women's clothing. Angela hesitated a moment, her face looked haunted. "You know, this is where it all started."

"What do you mean?" I asked.

She pointed inside. "I was in a clothing store similar to this one, when the men attacked me." She began to shake, her eyes filled with tears.

I clenched my fist. Seeing her like this upset me beyond belief. My first impulse was to sweep her into my arms and carry her away from all those memories as a storm carries away the heat from the day. I moved to put my arm around her, but Maritsa clucked her tongue and stepped between us.

Oh, yeah.

I'd forgotten, we were no longer at our secluded beach hideaway. We were in public, and certain rules had to be followed. I was slipping, and it was getting worse. "*Ahnjela*, it's okay, I can come back later to pick something up for you."

She shook her head and raised her chin, a forced smile creased her lips. "I can't let their terror rule my

94

life." She inhaled several times. "I can do this." She turned and entered the stall. Soon, Angela and Maritsa were the owners of fresh new clothes complete with a change for the next day. While they shopped, I stepped away to make a few purchases myself.

Sidig met us at the entrance to the market about an hour later. Angela and Maritsa had changed into brightly colored print robes, their hair bundled up in matching scarfs. They stashed the rest of their clothing in newly acquired travel bags. Even though Angela blended in with the shopping crowd, I continued to maintain a watchful eye on our surroundings.

"Do you have the tickets for the last boat this evening?" I asked Sidig.

He shook his head. "They're still repairing the storm damage. The first boat will not leave until ten-o'clock tomorrow morning,"

Damn, this was a massive delay that allowed Mustapha more time to locate us. He was out there somewhere, and would eventually search in Stone Town with its port and passage to the mainland.

We checked into a small hotel where we reserved three rooms, one for the women and one each for Sidig and myself. It was a medium-sized hotel with room service. I wanted to limit their exposure to the outside and had arranged for Maritsa and Angela to have dinner in their room.

I stopped by to make sure they had everything before turning in, only to meet Maritsa at the door. She had her new bag in her hand. "Oh, there you are, Grandson. I was coming to get you."

"What is this?" I eyed my grandmother with suspicion.

"I think you should have dinner with your fiancée."

"Bibi, she is not my—"

She waved her hand at me. "No need to explain. Take your time. Dinner is on the way." She held her hand out. "Let me have your key."

I was completely thrown off guard at her blatant meddling and surprised she did not come right out and tell me to switch rooms and spend the night. I pressed the key into her hand.

Angela stood by the window, a vision in her new long dress.

She chuckled. "I don't know what she said, but she must have had the last word."

"It would seem so."

There was a knock on the door, and a muffled voice said, "Room service."

A slender kid, with lots of acne, dressed in a hotel uniform, stood in the hallway. He had a rolling cart by his side. "You ordered dinner, Sir?" he asked politely.

"Yes, thank you," I stepped aside allowing him to push the cart in and station it near the wall. He uncovered the meal to reveal an overly large tureen full of soup with two bowls and spoons at its side.

What on Earth did Maritsa order?

Evening meals in Zanzibar consisted of fish, meat, vegetables and rice. Maybe, more was on the way. "Is this all we ordered?" I asked the server.

"Yes, *eet 'tis*." He smirked, bowed and quickly exited the room.

I placed the bowl on the table and pulled a chair out for Angela.

"I guess this is our dinner." She was as perplexed as I was. "Only soup?"

"Yes," I answered as I sat opposite her.

I filled the first bowl and passed it to Angela.

She took a sip and closed her eyes, savoring the taste. "Mmm, this is good. There is a lot of nutmeg in it. What's it called?"

"It's a typical Zanzibari dish." I tried a spoonful; bursts of nutmeg, vegetables and cream greeted my pallet. It tasted like the soup my mother used to make. "It's called nutmeg soup."

We ate for several minutes before I stopped and stared into space. An additional fact about nutmeg soup crossed my mind. I lowered my gaze to her half-empty bowl.

Alarmed, Angela stopped eating. "What's the matter?"

"It seems my grandmother didn't want to leave things to chance." I pointed to the bowl. "In Zanzibar, Nutmeg soup is considered an aphrodisiac."

She shook her head and giggled. Her mirth soon turned into full-out laughter. Once she settled down, she picked up her spoon and continued to eat. "An aphrodisiac? Really?"

Her glee was infectious. I found myself taking another spoonful and chuckling along with her. "Yes, they say, 'don't eat it while your husband is away'."

"That's crazy. But, it is good soup, and it is settling my nerves."

I held my hand out to her. "I'm sorry, this must have been a scary few days for you."

She sobered up and put her hand in mine. "Terrifying is a better description. Today, when you took me to that shop, all I could think about were those men who grabbed me. I froze, I literally froze. If you and Maritsa hadn't been there, I would've never gone inside. What's happening to me?"

I'd seen the condition she was in when I ransomed her. She was drugged out of her mind, her face bloodied and bruised. There was still vestiges of the bruising around her eye. The experience had to have terrorized her beyond belief. I'd helped other women with the same look on their face, and knew first hand, she would need time to recover. "You went through a horrible ordeal." I tightened my grip when tears threatened to flood her eyes. "You must give yourself time and a chance to heal, emotionally and physically."

She wiped her eyes, nodded and leaned closer. "Can you explain why they wanted to kidnap your fiancée?"

I was not sure where to begin. My dealings with Mustapha were a closely guarded secret, but she of all people, deserved to know the truth. I hesitated only because of my concern for her safety. "I mentioned earlier that I stole something from him. We've gone back and forth with our business dealings for years."

She was quiet for a moment. "Does this have something to do with the slave trade you mentioned?"

"*Ahnjela*, I really can't say much about it."

"What did you do to Mustapha?" Her voice was low with a hard edge to it.

She was not going to let this go. If I were her, I wouldn't either. This was as good a time as any to come clean. She deserved at least a part of the truth. My God, I'd pushed her through trees to get away from the maniac.

"*My* second business is smuggling. I stole his cargo of slave women."

She froze, her eyes fluttered as she processed what I'd just said. "You stole his cargo of *slave women*?"

I nodded. My pulse picked up speed. This discussion was becoming more difficult by the minute.

She continued. "And, the story you told me about being in the spice business?"

She was sharp and didn't miss a thing. "Is true. My spice business is a legitimate front to the less than legal enterprises I run."

"Oh." She seemed very uncomfortable, and I couldn't blame her one bit.

"*Ahnjela*, I tried hard to keep this all from you. I wanted you back home and safely away from this nightmare."

"What did you do with the women?" she whispered.

"I sent them to their villages." There was more to tell, but I refused to further jeopardize her life with information that would get her killed.

She got up, walked to the window and pulled the curtains aside to look out. I followed and stopped beside her. The sun was down, and the streetlights cast little halos of circles in the square. Tears formed at the sides of her eyes.

"*Ahnjela*, say something,"

She wiped her face. "Why?"

I wrapped my arms around her. "Because, I want to know what you are thinking."

She shook her head. "No. I meant why do you rescue the women? Why is this so important to you?"

The answer was close to my soul, and I never talked about it…not to anyone. She would be the first. "It's a long story." I felt her tense. "But, the short version is a cargo of slave women was transported through our port here in Zanzibar. A fight broke out between the traders, and it spilled into the market."

"You mean the shopping area we visited today?"

"Yes. Several shoppers were killed." I paused. It had happened four years ago, but it seemed like yesterday. "My mother and grandmother were hit by gunfire. The doctors were able to save my grandmother, but my mother died."

Angela turned in my arms. "Amir, I'm so sorry. I can't imagine how hard it was for you."

"It was some time ago," I hedge, resisting the urge to tell her more.

Her gaze was intense, like a bright beacon in the fog, piercing and clear. It felt like she could see straight into my soul. "So, you started a war with the traders?"

"Yes. As the years moved on, my war became more complicated and messy. Revenge would never bring my mother back, but at least I could put a dent in their operations and help the women as well."

Angela looked away stifling a sob. "You're an honorable man, Amir. I'm glad they made it home. You never hear those stories in the US." She sniffed. "I guess it's time for reality to kick in. I don't think I'm cut out to live this kind of life, and I don't want to be in the way of what you are doing here."

My heart stilled. I was not ready for this, even though I knew it had to happen. I pulled her to me. She molded into my arms, a perfect fit. "I'm sending you and Maritsa to safety." My voice caught. Every instinct in my body screamed to keep her close. "*Ahnjela*, they threatened your life twice. I would lose my mind if anything happened to you."

In my pocket was a ring box. I'd stopped at a jewel merchant to buy the ring, hoping for the chance to give it to her. Her eyes grew round when she saw its contents. "Is that a… diamond?"

It was a diamond surrounded by sapphires. "Be my fiancée, marry me."

"B-but you're sending me away!"

"It would be for a short while until this mess is cleared up."

"And, what about Zahra?"

"I don't want to marry Zahra. I love you."

There, I said it out loud for her to hear.

She was shaking like a palm tree in the wind but let me slip the ring on her finger. She stared at it then looked up at me. "I think we need some space. Amir, this is too much, too soon." She pulled the ring off and put it back in its box. Tears ran freely down her face. She hiccupped. "I can't survive a long-distance relationship."

She shattered my heart. I took several gulps of air before I could speak. "I understand."

"No, you don't. If you stay, we will…" She paused. "We will not make smart choices. I can't live in your world and mine is half the globe away. I'm afraid to let you into my heart any deeper, knowing it won't work out." She opened the door, sobbing.

"Please leave."

My room was a few steps down the hall, but it felt like a mile. My chest throbbed and ached to the beat of my heart. The pain was visceral, but I did not stop until I reached my door. Leaving was the right thing to do. We lived in separate worlds. Our lives were different. We had nothing in common other than one intense night of passion I would remember to my dying day.

I patted around for the key.

That's right, I gave it to my grandmother.

I knocked on the door. It took her a while, but she answered. She was stunned when she saw it was me. "What are you doing here?"

Her attitude spoke volumes about her expectation of not seeing me until the morning. "She kicked me out."

"Oh, the nutmeg soup hasn't started to work on her. She's a tricky one. She fights with herself too much. So, I had them put extra nutmeg in it."

"You what?" Was I hearing her correctly? My grandmother spiked the soup with extra aphrodisiac?

This took meddling to a whole new height. "Bibi, you shouldn't have—"

She held her hand up, cutting off my righteous indignation and wagged her finger at me. "You should be feeling the full effects, but here you stand. You are a waste of good nutmeg soup." Her finger turned toward Angela's door. "Go back!" She stepped inside the room and shut the door in my face.

I was stunned.

What the hell? Was I just kicked out of two rooms in the space of two minutes?

I went next door to Sidig's room and stood there talking myself out of knocking, asking for a pillow and a corner to lay my head on. An image of his stern, disapproving frown floated across my mind. I shook my head. There was no way I could explain to him what had just happened and maintain any semblance of self-respect. I went back to Angela's door prepared to confess to her what my grandmother was up to and...

The door opened.

Chapter 13

Angela

What was I thinking? I had just sent the sexiest man alive out the door. I knew this was the right thing to do. But, was my heart so fragile, I couldn't bear to be around him one more night before leaving?

Like it or not, this was shaping up to be the beginning of a long-distance relationship. I was never good at those and being with a man from Zanzibar was world-class long distance. I knew when I was in way over my head.

Smuggling? Slave trading? And don't forget kidnapping.

Rational Angela had a smug look on her face; leave it to her to remember the salient facts. DC had a set of knives in her hand. I stepped back from the door.

She's right, DC, back off, put the knives down.

I was good with this decision. If I could just keep telling myself this, I might believe it.

But, he looked so crushed when you gave the ring back. You know, the one big enough to put an Olympic size skating rink on?

Shut up, DC. Shut up! Rational Angela was actually screaming at DC.

Dear Jesus. I had never been so indecisive before. I was rooted to the spot, unable to move. It was DC who broke the stalemate. She took a running leap and jumped rational Angela. My God, she had her in a chokehold. They both went down in a jumble of hands and legs. DC screamed, *Open the damn door, you fool*.

My hand was a blur. It opened the door before another thought crossed my mind. Amir stood there in all his fine glory.

He stepped in, slammed the door shut, scooped me up into those brick hard arms and rained kisses on my lips. "*Ahnjela*, I can't let you go like this."

Blame it on the soup, or not, but right then and there in that space and time, my batteries were on full charge and ready to go. The man carried me to bed and pulled me in for a deeper, lingering kiss.

I came up for air. "I'm so sorry. I shouldn't have sent you away."

Those dark hooded eyes studied me like a religious zealot. "You had every right to do that. *Ahnjela*, I am not good for you. Your life would be in danger."

I put my finger against his lips. "I know, but tonight is for us. Tomorrow will come soon enough."

"I'll find you when this is all over, I swear it," he promised.

"Don't make promises you can't keep." I was realistic. Our affair would wind itself down, and we would go back to our lives with wistful memories of these two days together.

I ran my finger down his chest. His loose, pale grey top was rumpled in places. "Stand up, strip for me," I said.

A myriad of emotions ran across his face. The bulge at his crotch jumped. "As you wish, but I must warn you, my grandmother spiked the soup."

"What? The aphrodisiac soup?" I used air quotes on the word aphrodisiac.

He nodded. "She had them lay the nutmeg on thick."

"You have got to be kidding me."

What is it with these people and that soup?

"You ate it too. You seem to be fine. I mean you walked out of the room. How good could this soup be?"

I looked down at the bulge at his crotch.

Yeah, and he has been quite successful at doing that on his own without the help of nutmeg soup.

He swallowed hard. "Believe me when I tell you the soup was *very* good." He had a predatory look in his eyes.

"Then get up and take your clothes off. Do it slow and sexy."

I have never said or done anything like this in my life. Maybe it was the extra nutmeg.

Then DC whispered in my ear. What she suggested was naughty and wicked. The cool part was that rational Angela was on board. Jeez getting those two on the same page was like a miracle. I chuckled and held my hand up.

He was in the process of pulling off his shirt. Corded muscles flexed and flowed as the shirt inched up over his head then landed in a heap on the floor.

My mouth watered. "Good, very good"

Was that my voice?

It was low, husky and sexy.

I may have to get the recipe for that soup.

I stood up and pushed him against the wall. I ran my hands up his fabulous washboard abs. When I got to his shoulders, I leaned close, rubbing every inch I owned against his hard body. I whispered in his ear. "Sweetheart, if we are going to do this, we might as well do this all the way."

"What do you mean, habibi?" His voice a deep rumble I felt straight to my bones.

"You move in for the night. Go get your things, and we will do this like a normal couple. You know, really get to know each other."

He chuckled. "Know each other?"

I nodded. "Yeah, warts and all."

The look on his face was priceless. "I don't have warts. At least I don't think I do." He paused. "What are warts?"

I walked over to the door. "It is a figure of speech. We'll do the things normal people do. You know, have our regular bedtime routine. Use the bathroom, take a shower, brush our teeth put on pajamas. I do my hair, you know, normal stuff."

His smile was crooked. "You mean, see if we can stand each other's eccentric behavior?"

I nodded.

"Woman, you scare me." He opened the door, looked down the hall at his room then closed it.

I crossed my arms. "Is there a problem?"

His jaw twitched a couple of times before he answered, "Don't laugh but my grandmother put me out, and I can't go back."

This family had me completely baffled. "Why on Earth not?"

I could tell he was uncomfortable with this discussion. His shoulders slumped, and he looked away refusing to make eye contact. Yeah, this topic bothered him. He wrestled with his conscience for a few seconds before he blurted out. "She said I was a waste of Nutmeg soup and sent me back over here."

The mirth started from my chest. It bubbled up in a fast-moving wave making me vibrate like my favorite dildo I keep hidden in the closet. I could not help it. I was laughing out loud before I could stop myself.

"I told you not to laugh."

I pushed him aside and opened the door. "Oh, for goodness sake, move out of the way."

"No, wait, I have to check the hallway…"

I was out the door and down the hall in a flash. This was way too good. I knocked on the door. Maritsa yelled out a string of words in Kiswahili. I didn't understand a thing, but I knew the sound of a perturbed, black woman when I heard it. Words streamed from her mouth at a steady clip as she stomped toward the door. I looked back at Amir and winked. He'd managed to put his shirt

108

back on and stood at our door with his arms crossed. I pointed at his crotch and mimed that he should cover it. He glanced down at the bulge in his pants, jumped and covered his crotch, his face an indignant mask of fury. I laughed again. This was delightful.

Maritsa flung the door open. "Amir!" She stopped when she saw it was me. Her jaw dropped open and just as quickly snapped shut. She smiled sweetly. "Daughter, what can I do for you?"

I gave her my brightest smile. "Well..." I gestured toward Amir. He was leaning against the doorjamb glaring at us both. "Thank you so much for the soup. Amir and I are going to have a sleepover." I stole a glance back at him; his eye had developed a tick. "I just came over to get his things. You know, his toothbrush, toiletries and a change of clothes."

She ushered me into the room, her lips curved into a wicked grin. "Let me help you pack."

Soon, the bag was packed, and I was back out in the hallway. Maritsa gave me a big hug. "You good, *gal*. Keep him happy."

"Maritsa—"

"Call me Bibi. It means grandmother." She winked.

"Okay, Bibi. I will do my best, tonight."

She clucked her tongue and was positively beaming.

I returned to our room with the bag and put it on one of the two chairs. "Well now, that was refreshing."

Amir stood there, clearly upset. "*Ahnjela*, what were you thinking? The hallway is not secure. We should not telegraph to the world what we are doing."

109

"Your grandmother is a delight. And, no one is going to see and arrest us."

He glanced over at the door and relaxed a little. "I'm glad you think so. And, when the police knock down the door, I will let you explain everything to them." He shook his head and came over to put his arms around me. "But, you know, this means *we* are a done deal."

I raised an eyebrow. "What do you mean by *we*?"

"She wants you to call her Bibi. I think she approves of you."

"Good, I approve of her too." I wiggled out of his embrace.

"Where are you going?"

"I call first dibs on the shower. Oh, and when we're done bathing, I plan to ride you like a horse and not let you up until you beg for mercy."

He stared at me. I guessed he was working on the translation of my English to Kiswahili. In any case, he finally got the message and found his voice. "I don't beg for anything."

Chapter 14

*A*ngela

I felt grimy from head to toe. I had spent the morning in a rain-soaked jungle and the afternoon in a dusty market. A hot shower was mandatory. The bathroom was small with everything fitting into space the size of a broom closet. But, it was a private bathroom and had a small shower. I happily put this in the plus column.

Amir came in and knocked on the stall. "Can I help you?"

There was no room for shenanigans as the shower stall was too small, but I could use the help rinsing my hair. "Come on in, but understand, no sexual acrobatics."

He dominated the space. His shoulders were the width of the stall, and his head was higher than the door. "What makes you think I'm into acrobatics?" he teased.

I snorted and glanced down. His hard-on was up close and personal. Maybe letting him in here with all of his man-flesh was not the best idea. Waiting to finish my hair and squeeze out of this space was going to be difficult. I sighed and turned back into the hot spray. "This shower is the size of a postage stamp. If we get

111

wedged into a compromised position, I'm gonna let you yell for Maritsa," I passed the soap. "Now, help me wash my hair, so we can get out of here."

"Yes, ma'am."

Soon, I had a nice lather on my head. I shivered in delight. His hands were like magic; they rubbed and kneaded the tension from my scalp. With my hair washed and rinsed into tight ringlets, he turned his attention to other areas. My back came first, then my thighs and legs. Each pass of his soaped hands a study in sensual delight. Oh heavens, I really needed to keep this man.

Once he finished, it was my turn to work on him. "Hand me the soap and turn around."

"You're bossy," he complained as he followed orders.

"I think you like that about me."

I lathered his tight backside. Goodness, this man was put together nicely. Muscles stretched taut over well-defined shoulders. His rear was high, tight and right. I ran my hands down his thighs and he shuddered. "*Ahnjela*, what are you doing?"

"It's called bathing."

"I call it torture."

He spun around and scooped me up for a searing kiss. The combination of the water cascading over our bodies, and his hands rubbing my back, sent my head spinning.

I rose up on my toes and whispered in his ear. "One taste is all I want."

"What?"

"Lean back, and I'll show you." I pushed him against the wall and got down on my knees.

He swallowed hard, and all his equipment seemed to rise higher. I began at his flared tip and slowly circled it with my hand cupping and gently kneading his sack. My tongue flicked down his length, and when I reached the base, I sucked in and out like he was a lollipop. I was merciless in my ministrations. The warm water hit us, creating a steam-filled space where his heavy breathing and my sucking were drowned out by the sound of the hot spray.

"*Ahnjela*," he whispered.

I took one last hard draw on his cock and stood up with a big Cheshire cat grin on my face.

"Please don't stop."

"Are you begging?"

He shuddered and worked his throat; his Adam's apple was almost a blur. He snaked his arm around me and pulled me in for another mind-numbing kiss. "Woman, you test me." He lifted me up. "Wrap your legs around my waist."

I hesitated. "Um, I don't think…"

He pulled my right leg up. I lifted my left, and it hit the wall. He turned to give us more space, but my knee connected with the wall again, and I hissed in pain. He turned one more time, but the space would not fit us.

"Arggg…" his growl was guttural. It rumbled through his chest. He put me down and leaned his forehead against mine; his breath came out in hard bursts.

"I tried to warn you about the lack of room for serious canoodling."

The spray of the water sputtered and turned cold. I squealed and reached for the knob to turn it off. "I guess we're done here. The heater for this shower was not meant for long, hot naughty baths."

His response was raw and visceral, "I want you."

I patted him on his chest and slipped out of the stall. "You're a big boy. You can wait."

My hair, on the other hand, could not wait. I had a short window of time before it became a gigantic puffball. Making small twists all over my head tamed it. At least for a while. I was in a humid environment, and any attempted at taming was a lesson in patience mixed with a healthy amount of futility.

I wrapped a towel around myself, stood in front of the bathroom mirror and brush through my hair. He stationed himself behind me and ran his fingers through the coils interfering with my strokes. He held my curls like they were the finest silk, making it difficult for me to complain.

"It's so soft and beautiful; May I try?"

I snorted. "Are you serious?"

"Yes." His hands twitched in anticipation.

My mind tripped over the notion of a hard-bodied man asking to do my hair. I was intrigued but could not let him win too easily. "I know better than to let you mess with my hair."

"You let me mess with it last night."

He had a point. "Touché, sir." I passed a comb to him. "Here you go."

Amir wrapped a towel around his waist and led me to one of the chairs in the main room. He was going to comb my hair. What a novel experience and surprisingly sexy too.

He expertly parted my hair in an unusual pattern. I reached up to feel the rows, and he batted my hand away. "Are you braiding my hair?"

"Yes. You said you wanted it braided."

I turned to look at him. "Have you braided hair before?" In the short time, we were together, he'd showed many sides of his personality. I never expected this to be one of his talents.

He shook his head. "No, not really. I watched it done. Now, stop moving and look straight ahead."

He swung me around and had me face the bed. "Did you watch your sisters?"

"Oh, no. I watched the ladies in my..." He paused. "In my staff... They have daughters."

There was something he was not telling me, but I didn't press the issue as his hair braiding skills intrigued me. He moved fast and soon my hair was neatly cornrowed and braided into a bun in the back of my head.

I dashed to the mirror in the bathroom. The cornrows zig-sagged diagonally over the crown of my head. They were neat, beautifully designed and most importantly, not too tight.

"If you hadn't just done this, I wouldn't have believed it."

He slowly sauntered in behind me. "You like it?"

I patted my new hairdo. "You betcha." I gave him a steely stare. "Don't you ever let any woman know you can do this."

"Huh?"

"I mean it, Amir bin Sultan, if this gets out, I will have to fight off a flock of women." I clicked off the attributes. "Guy can dance, out-of-this-world kisser, world-class lover AND does hair? You, sir are a keeper."

He stood there with a big grin on his face. "So, you *will* keep me?"

I turned back to admire my hair. Oh yes, he'd just upped the ante. Despite my earlier resolve to build a wall, and go off alone with my sweet memories, he was breaking down my defenses. "I'm seriously thinking about it."

"Now, back to that part about being a world-class lover." He grabbed my hand, swooped me up and carried me to the bed.

"Amir, make love to me like tomorrow will never come." I meant it. Live in the moment became my mantra. The morning would bring my departure and eventual heartache. I'd found something special in Amir, the man who turned personal tragedy into hope for so many. I could easily fall in love with him if I stayed. But, would we survive our forced separation?

His eyes took on that extra dark quality. The girls back home called it, 'bedroom eyes.' "Your wish is my command." The smoke in his eyes was hypnotic. I stared, caught in its depths. His kiss left me panting for more. I straddled his thighs, my towel slipped exposing my breasts and puddled around our hips. His lips drew a hot path down my body, lingering for a while at my nipples. My hands tangled in the curls on his head holding him close. I did not want him to move. Yesterday we touched and explored, his attention to my body was pure devotion. Tonight, with the effects of the soup washing over me, I wanted to play.

The scent of nutmeg and musk circled us in its snare and surrounded us in a cocoon of carnal desire and heat.

"*Ahnjela*," he moaned.

I positioned myself over him and spread my legs until he slowly entered me. "Yes, Amir?"

I rose halfway, then lowered myself again. His hands gripped my hips. "*Ahnjela*," his voice cracked.

Our tongues tangled; the taste of nutmeg filled my mouth and went straight to all my erogenous nerve endings. One heat-filled stroke turned into two more. I nibbled his earlobe and whispered, "Say my name again." My tone was breathy and sweet and wrong as can be.

Oh, hell yeah; he's gonna beg, DC whispered in my ear.

His breathing was ragged and uneven; his eyes were dark coals. "*Ahnjela*, what are you doing to me?"

My movements were slow and methodical, driving him crazy. "Making you beg." I rocked back and forth undulating to the beat of our hearts. "We will remember tonight for years to come."

His voice rasped, "Don't stop."

Lightly, I ran my nails down his chest. He shuddered, and I felt his quaking throughout my entire body. It centered right there where we connected. I clamped down on him and rode his goodness. He sucked my nipples like they were sweet fruit and brought them up to pert peaks. "Are you begging?"

He nodded. "Yes."

That was all I needed to hear. I picked up speed giving him a *hard, grinding, knock-boots kinda ride*. I threw my arms in the air and arched back riding the fire that consumed us both.

"Wrap your legs around my waist," he ordered.

I was out of my mind in lust, granting any command. I did as instructed. No sooner than I had my legs around him, he bucked into me, twisted, and I was on my back with my legs pointed toward the ceiling. He delivered searing bone on bone strokes—the kind a girl dreams about a hot lover giving. He sent me into the stratosphere as he slammed into me over and over.

"Amir, Amir," I chanted his name holding on to his back, feeling his muscles work into me like a machine on overdrive.

This was an all-time high, a dime store cigarette with a hashish kicker. Only, this hash was laced with nutmeg and spice. He worked me up and over into nirvana. I yelled his name my voice low and throaty. My orgasm triggered his, and we came together in a crescendo of heat, sweat and joy.

"*Ahnjela*," he croaked my name one final time as he shuddered and delivered pulsing goodness deep in my core. We were sweaty, our hands rubbing, stroking, soaking up every ounce of sexual energy like it was our last.

Amir never ceased to amaze me in his ability to corral my two personalities and lavish them with so much passion and joy. He understood us and made us happy and whole. DC hummed and nibbled on chocolate Amir shaped brownies, a satisfied smile creased her lips. She broke off a large piece and handed it to Rational Angela who sat next to her fanning her face. He could get them on the same page like nobody's business.

*****

*A*mir

We made love to the wee hours of the morning, quietly caressing and holding each other, desperate for the night to never end. Angela set me on a combustible rush like no other. One look in her hazel colored eyes, and I knew if she wanted us wild and crazy or cool and easy. All it took was a tilt of her head, a flutter of a lash or a hard stare combined with a flare of her nostrils. She was multifaceted, passionate and uniquely Angela. All of her parts created one woman that I loved, craved.

119

The city stirred to life while we held onto our last few hours together. Sounds of the early morning fish market filtered through the window. Small trucks carrying their load in from the sea trundled pass the hotel; their deep-throated engines rattled the walls and windows alike.

She snuggled into me like the first night I brought her home, her face relaxed and serene. I pulled her closer and inhaled her jasmine-scented goodness. A sense of peace settled over me like a blanket warmed by the Zanzibarian sunshine.

"Hmmm." A satisfied hum escaped my lips.

I stopped myself to keep from disturbing her. Honestly, I wanted to watch her sleep and imagine we were in a time capsule. One where I did not have to send her away, and we could spend our days loving each other without regrets or secrets.

Her eyes fluttered open; their intense hazel gaze flickered across my face. "Good morning."

Her soft sexy voice, so full of sleep, brought a smile to my lips. "Good morning to you beautiful."

She hummed and stretched; her body pulled taught against mine then relaxed. Every cell I owned stood up at attention. I could easily lay here all day, and hold her, talking about her dreams. "If you could do anything today, what would it be?" I asked.

She shrugged her shoulders. "Hold your hand and take a long walk on the beach. What would you do?"

I picked up her hand and studied her long, elegant fingers. A surgeon's hand. "I would take these hands and swing you across a dance floor. I know you like dancing."

She nodded and sighed. "There is never enough time in the day to do the things we enjoy doing." She lifted her head. "As soon as I get home, I'll have to catch up on the paperwork for my intern program and prepare for upcoming surgeries."

She was a busy woman with a full life in another country on the other side of the world. Even then, I thought I heard a small amount of regret in her voice.

"At some point, we must take time for ourselves." I don't believe I'd just said that. Maritsa spent hours repeating those words to me. I would waive her away, ignoring her advice and continue to work."

Angela made a sad face and tucked her arms back around my chest. "Has she met my mother? I swear they think alike,"

My laughter came from the ache in my soul. The truths we received from our elders should one day sift into our lives and turn us in another direction. Yet, here we are, tucked in this small room wishing time would stand still and give us a chance to talk for hours about the little things that made us happy.

I kissed away the salty tears that leaked from the corners of her eyes. "Don't cry, habibi,"

Her lips found mine, and the morning, along with our problems, faded away.

The sun came up too soon; its rays flooded the room with amber light and warmth, announcing louder than a bullhorn at the morning fish market that a new day had begun. For one brief moment, I hated that sun. I was right where I wanted to be, tangled up with this beautiful woman, our bodies melded as one. But, time stood still for no one, and all good things had to end.

Angela sighed, her voice heavy with regret. "We have to get up."

"I know."

*****

*A*ngela

My heart ached as I pulled on my clothes. I wanted our conversation to go on forever prolonging the illusion we were a normal couple discussing our plans for the day. Talking with Amir felt natural; our conversation flowed smoothly like we'd known each other for years. We held each other and whispered our deepest wishes and desires instead of admitting our fears. Mine was that I would never see him again after today. The reality of this fear greeted us along with the glare of the morning sun as we left the hotel.

Amir and Sidig escorted us to the dock. Both Maritsa and I wore traditional Zanzibari dresses; they flowed out behind us as we walked. Maritsa was ahead of us but glanced back occasionally with a contented smile.

The boat was anchored at the end of the pier rolling and pitching in the heavy post-storm swells. I pinched my nose; the entire area reeked of fish, diesel fuel and trash. Dead trees littered the area where the wind dumped them. Birds flew in and out diving for food amid the damage and detritus. Their cries mingled with the sound of the surf and the strong breeze that flow onto the island.

We walked in silence; I did not trust myself to speak, a tight knot lodged in my throat. I moved beside him, keeping my back straight and my eyes forward praying to my ancestors for a small amount of emotional control.

He held my hand "Stay safe, *Ahnjela*. Know that I love you."

Tears welled at the corners of my eyes. I sniffled and lifted my chin, determined to keep my promise not to cry. One glance at his dreamy bedroom eyes, and I wished I could turn back the clock and start the morning again. Stepping on that boat and watching him recede in the distance would be the end of our romance.

"Goodbye, Amir, please take care of yourself." My heart broke. Saying the word *goodbye,* felt so permanent.

"Go, now. It's time to board," he said, his voice a whisper I barely heard over the sound of the engines.

Sidig carried our small bags and boarded first; his traditional robes flapped in the breeze exposing his pants and long shirt underneath. He was our escort and protection. Once we were safely in Dar es Salaam, he was scheduled to return. He set our bags down and turned to help Maritsa across. I followed behind her, my steps felt like lead as every cell in my body screamed in defiance. The boarding plank bounced and jostled from the boat bobbing in the rough surf. I stumbled back onto the pier. Amir caught me and gave me a reassuring squeeze before he helped me across. The wind picked up, blowing dark grey clouds overhead obscuring the sunlight but not the tears of my heart.

Gods this hurt.

I stood at the bow, staring at him. He seemed so lost and alone. Even his loose, tan pants and shirt drooped off his body like they were two sizes too large. My eyes misted; I wanted to run to him straighten his clothes and hug him one last time.

The horn blew, the engine revved with a deep, earthy growl, and we slowly pulled away. People milled around him, but we never lost eye contact.

Men pushed their way through the crowd knocking slower people out of the way. They stopped behind Amir, threw a sack over his head and hit him. My scream was lost in the wail of the horn. I got Sidig's attention, then threw one leg over the railing to jump overboard and rescue him. Sidig pulled me back.

"No, I need to help him." I clawed at Sidig's hand, but he held me tight. "Angela, you would be killed in the waves."

"We have to save him," I protested.

"There is no *we*. You are getting on the plane to America. I'll handle this," he said.

I stopped struggling. He was not surprised at all. "You know where they're taking him, don't you?"

His eyes betrayed him.

"Then tell me where."

He shook his head.

"Why? Why won't you tell me?" I yelled.

His jaw clenched. "Amir didn't want you to know because it would endanger your life."

That stopped me. Cold dread slithered to the base of my spine-. "Tell me anyway."

He sighed and looked at the receding port. In the distance, a truck with Amir inside pulled away. "They want his harem."

I knew I did not hear that right. "Say that again."

"They're taking him to his harem."

Chapter 15

*A*ngela

*H*e. Has. A. Harem?

Of course, he does. He is the sultan's son, and they tend to have harems. What the *hell* could I do with that kind of information? And, for that matter, why would it endanger me?

It's times like this when a girl understands the full measure of her character. Rational Angela said, '*cut and run.*' DC said, '*go get your man, take over the harem and make it yours.*'

Yeah, that's the stuff real women do.

My mind swung in another direction because it could not process the '*take over the harem*' comment. What does a man do with a harem in this day in age? I could not even imagine. Where does he keep them? Does he sleep with all of them? *Did I care?*

Yes, I cared. That was the problem. I had been dodging my real feelings about him for a while. He was everything I'd wanted, caring, thoughtful, strong and sexy. He rocked my world like no other man. My big stumbling block was our lives were so different as well as so far apart. I was not leaving Washington DC, and he had important work to do here. I would never demand he stop helping the women to be with me, and there was no way we could survive a long-distance relationship. Having a harem added an insane amount of complication, even I could not wrap my brain around. Leaving was the best option for both of us even though my heart screamed to find another way.

I stared into space with my mind at full throttle. The boat bounced and pitched, its engines labored to push us through the swells. My emotions were like the sea. Turbulent. Erratic. Each option I considered was knocked around then discarded like flotsam in the water. Reconciling the internal war blazing in my head took all my concentration rendering Sidig's words indistinct, hazy.

"Angela, Angela," he yelled, his hand flashed back and forth in front of my face.

I shuddered and blinked to clear the molasses that so generously gummed up my brain. "Yes, I'm sorry. What were you saying?"

"It's not what you think."

"What's not what I think?"

"His harem."

******

*A*mir

My focus had slipped one time too many, and I knew it. Being tied up in the back of this truck was my punishment. Mustapha must have been watching the port. With my attention completely focused on Angela, grabbing me was a no-brainer. I was so disgusted; I didn't even put up a fight.

They'd covered my head with a sack, tied my hands behind my back and thrown me on the floor of the truck. We left the port, and soon the slower city traffic changed to the lighter traffic of the countryside. The truck made a hard right turn. I slid and hit the side, pain lanced through my shoulder. My head was splitting thanks to the hit I took. The road smoothed out, and the truck rumbled on picking up speed. This was going to be a long dusty ride. If we were heading out of town, there was only one place we were going. *My harem.*

The question was how did he find its location?

I knew what Mustapha wanted. I'd kept the information from Angela for their safety and hers. Anyone with this information could be used to endanger the harem. The women had gone through so much trauma; I did not want to be the cause of anymore.

After my mother's death, I'd vowed to stop as much of it as I could. I had spent the last three years pirating Mustapha's shipments of slave women to the Middle East. I would let his other shipments of guns and drugs alone but intercepted the boats loaded with women before they left port.

Each time my methods changed preventing him from discovering my identity. My goal was never to let him know I was the one behind the thefts. Once I had the women, I took them to a compound deep in the heart of Zanzibar where they would rest while I arranged transport back to their different villages.

Despite my best intentions, not all their stories had happy endings. Some girls would not be accepted back home, especially the ones who were pregnant. They were kicked out of the village and left to live their lives with no support. I was not able, in good conscience, to leave them to fend for themselves and would take them back.

I educated them, trained them, prepared them to live and thrive anywhere they wished. Some would leave, others chose to stay. I did not trust the location of their compound to anyone other than Sidig; which meant, their security had to be handled by the women. They were trained in weapons and hand-to-hand combat. They also received extensive education, so they could teach themselves and their children. A small clinic with trained staff was created for medical needs. The compound soon became a self-contained village deep in the interior of the island. They named it *Sultan's Harem*, ignoring my objections on this matter.

This latest shipment of women was different. It had twice the number, more than thirty. It smelled like a setup, but I took the bait, anyway. I rescued them before they were loaded onto the boat and sent them to the harem to wait for transportation home. Mustapha was due to make millions for them. Yeah, he was pissed at me.

The sack that covered my head was scratchy but loosely woven. I caught glimpses of the other men in the back of the truck. There was a child with them as well. She whimpered with each jarring bump in the road.

The truck hit a few potholes and jigged to the right before it continued. I felt every rut and pit right through the floor of the truck. The heat and humidity exponentially increased the farther inland we rode.

I shifted and sat up against the wall knowing we had a long and uncomfortable drive ahead. The child sniffled and began to cry.

"Stop her crying," one of the men grated.

"Leave her alone." The sack muffled my voice.

Someone smacked me on the side of my head. "Stay out of it." His deep base voice carried above the noise of the truck.

"Ephrim, is that you?" I asked. The man did not answer. I continued, "I recognize your voice."

He abruptly pulled the sack from my head. I blinked to counter the effects of the sunlight beaming through the windows of the truck.

Mustapha's son, Ephrim, sat in front of me, and he was not happy with my capture. He was taller and broader shouldered than his father. Instead of close-cropped hair, his was locked and long gathered with a cord at the nape of his neck.

One quick look around and I saw that someone had fitted a low bench on either side of the truck bed. The bench on the left held three men dressed in military fatigues. Their guns sat loosely in their hands. On the right sat Ephrim and a fourth man who had a meaty hand wrapped around a little girl's arm. Her bright yellow dress was torn and dirty.

I realized it was Talima, the eight-year-old daughter of the head of my security team. They must have captured her during the raid yesterday.

I leaned forward. "Talima, where is your mother?"

She sniffed and pointed toward the cab of the truck. "Up front."

The man, I think his name was Aubrey, tightened his grip on her arm. "Silence, girl."

He shook her, and she screamed, "Sultan, help me."

All the women in the harem and their children called me, 'Sultan' even when I asked them not to. I clenched my teeth the second he touched her. There was no reason to treat her this way. He was a dead man once I got Talima safely away. I turned to Ephrim. "You know better than this. Let her come to me. He's hurting her."

Ephrim typically stayed away from this side of his father's business. It did not make sense for him to be here. He motioned for Aubrey to let her go.

Aubrey gave her arm one more squeeze before releasing her. Talima yanked herself away and scrambled over to me. I wished I could hold and comfort her, but my hands were still tied.

Talima shivered like the vanilla leaves in a storm. She seemed worn down and frail as she tucked her arms around me and sobbed. Her hair, cornrowed in a diagonal zigzag across the crown of her head, was frayed at the edges, some braids pulled out of their row. I had watched her mother do her hair a couple of nights ago and was fascinated by the intricacy of the design. Now the child sat by my side disheveled and frightened.

I flexed my hands testing the rope that bound them. It was solid and would not break easily. My only option was to wait for them to make a mistake, which would eventually happen. They should have never invaded my home. Mustapha would pay for this.

"Talima, it'll be okay," I reassured her.

She shook her head. "They hit Momma. They want her to show them to your harem."

Now, I was certain we were heading to the harem. Talima's mother, Olanda, was one of the strongest and most capable of the security team. She did not give up easily and had probably broken a few heads during the attack. They'd found and threatened Talima to get her mother's cooperation. Olanda would show them the way to the compound but not the most direct route. We had safeguards in place just in case something like this happened. Attacking the compound would not be so easy.

******

Angela

"Sidig, what do you mean they will find resistance at the compound?" He'd just finished telling me about Amir's harem. We were almost to the port of Dar es Salam. The three of us sat in a booth with a table, Sidig on one side with Maritsa and myself on the other.

The boat slowed to one third its speed. Its engines rumbled and sent deep-throated vibrations through the deck. Passengers gathered by the rail waiting to be the first to disembark. They bounced and bobbed but kept their footing as the boat moved through the heavy waves. Maritsa calmly sipped tea, but I was green from the rough crossing. Somehow, I'd managed to keep my breakfast down.

"Amir left orders for them to shoot to kill."

It was hard to hear him over the deep drone of the engines. "Let me get this straight," My jaws clinched punctuating each syllable. "He rescued women, created a haven for those who could not return home, armed them to the teeth with guns..." My fist connected with the table making Sidig jump. "And, he told them to shoot and kill anyone who came near?" My voice went up two octaves. It echoed off the metal wall of the stall.

Sidig waived his hands to calm me. "Shhhh...people may hear you."

"On what planet does any of this make sense?" I asked, my voice lower yet strained.

Last night Amir had told me about rescuing women in an attempt to slow down the slave trade that plagued the island. He said they sent the women home. This was a preferred outcome; I even felt it was admirable someone cared enough to do something about the problem. What pissed me off was the part he left out. The part that included a harem…a militarized harem; one with shoot to kill orders.

"If they see Amir strolling up, won't they let him in?"

He shook his head. "Only if he approaches from a certain path. If he walks up to the compound from any other direction…" Sidig stopped and pursed his lips. "They have orders to shoot."

"Are you telling me he's deliberately going to approach from the wrong way knowing they will shoot him?"

This was a death sentence. I was on my way home believing we would never see each other again. I fully expected him to marry Zahra and go on with his life. Yes, it would be heartbreaking, but at least he would be alive. What Sidig was saying was difficult to believe.

He nodded. "If any of us are captured and unable to communicate with the compound, the security team had orders to shoot first."

My world spiraled out of its orbit, and it seemed the chaos that sent it there reigned supreme. But, I refused to accept the finality in his statement. There had to be something we could do. "If Amir can't contact them, maybe you can."

Sidig shook his head. "They won't listen to me."

134

"What? Don't you have a secret code or something for just these situations?" I tightened my fists in frustration instead of banging them on the table.

"They will only listen to the Sultan..." He paused and eyed me closely. "I have an idea. It's a long shot but..." He shook his head. "Never mind, I have orders to send you home."

Send me home and leave him in danger?

I could not believe my ears. All at once, it was clear to me that returning to my safe, stable life and not attempting to help was wrong in so many ways. I cared too much about him to leave without doing something. "You're going to ignore those orders. So, spill it."

His mouth was drawn in a thin line. I guessed he was weighing his options. Finally, he hit the table so hard it rattled. "Amir is going to kill me."

"At least he'll be alive to do so," I countered.

"Okay, pretty much everyone in the harem has heard about you by now." He gave Maritsa a pointed look. She ignored him and continued to sip her tea.

Great, just great. I've landed on an island full of gossips.

I rubbed my eyes. They stung, and I was sure I had bags under them large enough to hold next week's groceries. "Tell me, what's your plan?" My voice was surprisingly calm and controlled.

"In our country, the Sultan's wife controls the harem. We simply tell them you are the Sultana, and you order them not to shoot him."

My mouth moved, but nothing came out. It froze in shock at the enormity of his suggestion. "You want me to lie to them?"

Maritsa who had been quiet this whole time piped up. "No lie, you're Sultana," she chuckled.

I ignored her. "The harem you describe is not a *traditional harem*."

"If they don't strictly follow the rules of a harem, then me giving them a call saying I am the Sultana won't work."

He pulled out his cell phone and began to dial. "That's why it's a long shot."

Chapter 16

*A*ngela

We reached Dar es Salaam less than a half hour later. This port was different from the one at Stone Town. It was larger, more congested with cars and people. The oppressive heat and humidity made it feel like I was walking through a giant fish bowl. Long gone were the sweet smell of spices and more cooling breezes of the Indian Ocean trade winds.

Sidig rented a car and drove us to a relative's house to drop off Maritsa. It sat in a quiet neighborhood located in the south of the city. She gave me a long, hard hug before she went inside. "Go and get 'im back. You good gal and smart. I know you will do it." He must have handed her the ring box before we boarded the boat because she held it up in front of me. "This will be waiting for you when you return."

I gave her a tired smile and kissed her on both cheeks. "Yes, ma'am."

We drove to a park and Sidig made the call. He'd tried calling from the boat, but there was no reception.

The park was near a cell tower, and we crossed our fingers in hopes it would work.

The wait was nerve-wracking. I rubbed my hands to hide the tremors running through them. "Sidig, what we're doing is a deliberate lie. I'm not good at this,"

His fingers beat an irritated staccato on the steering wheel. "Angela, you tell them you're the Sultana and order them not to shoot Amir. Then we pick up your cousin, and I take you both to the airport and put you on the plane."

On the surface, the plan was simple. The problem was it hinged on my ability to convince a stranger, to listen to me. I always got caught when I lied. Small inconsequential fibs were not so bad, but this was a big whopper. There was no way they would believe me and too much was at stake. Amir's life depended on my ability to convince them to change his order. I stared at the phone, shaking like a leaf, praying my voice would work when the time came.

The call went through ratcheting my pulse up several notches. Sidig spoke in Kiswahili for several minutes. I heard the names 'Sultan and Sultana' a couple of times. Finally, he gave me the phone.

A female voice on the other end spoke. "*Haloo.*"

I dragged in a lung full of oxygen and put on my best professional voice. "Hello, may I speak to the head of security."

There was a pause before the woman answered, "You *spek* English like an *Amerikaan.*"

Oh boy, here we go.

"Yes, I do. This is Angela Jones. Whom am I speaking with?"

Her accent was thick. "Dis is Grace, security head. I will *spek* to you because I was told Sultan pick a Sultana who *spek* English with *Amerikaan* accent."

Well now, all praises to the accuracy of the island gossips.

The knots in my stomach loosened and my voice steadied. "Yes. We have a problem. Someone took the Sultan and is heading your way."

"We were wondering if something was wrong when we were not able to get Sultan on *de* phone after *de* storm. Thought it problem *wit* his cell."

Their assumptions were understandable. They could never have predicted the attack on the house. "He was taken by Mustapha. We think they are going to attack the…" I paused, still having trouble with this whole 'harem' thing. "We think they want to attack your compound."

"*Tank* you for *de* warning. We will prepare."

I crossed my fingers with the next request. "One more thing. When the Sultan approaches from the wrong direction. Don't shoot him."

"He gave us *de* orders himself. On what authority do you have to change orders?"

I looked at Sidig and he nodded. One breath later, it came out of my mouth. "I am the Sultana, and I'm changing his orders."

The pause on the other line was so long; I thought she'd hung up on us. Finally, she spoke, "If dis is what the Sultana wishes."

"Yes, Grace; it is."

She agreed to my request. *She believed me.* His orders were officially changed and my task complete. The next step was to pick Queisha up at the hotel, leave the country and return to my life. Cut and run. But, as I held that phone, my chest grew heavy, a lump formed in my throat. I'd left him on the dock; his expression was devastating like he'd lost a piece of his soul. He was so focused on me, his *Ahnjela,* he did not see Mustapha coming. The image of him throwing the sack over Amir's head burned deep in my mind. They took him right in front of my eyes, and there was nothing I could do.

Truthfully, I'd fallen in love with him the first time he swooped me up in his arms. His soul-searing determination and drive captivated me. We could talk for hours like we'd known each other for years. His heart was good, and he put his life on the line for his beliefs. More importantly, he made me feel like the queen of the Nile. Cherished. His kisses convinced me to push past my fear of heights and climb a tree. Hell, I jump out of that tree too. I lapped up every ounce of sugar he passed my way and wanted more. There was no way I was getting on that plane and leaving him to his fate. Yes, this was love. Nothing else would turn my head away from home, work and responsibilities.

With my decision made, my pulse slowed and my head cleared. The cut and run option was off the table and taking over the harem suddenly made a whole lot of sense. Static filled the phone line, Grace's voice faded in and out. I added one last demand before we lost the call. "I will be coming too, so don't shoot me either."

There was something that sounded like a harsh chuckle on the other end of the line. Or, maybe she was coughing. In any case, her words were clear enough. "Come see your harem, Sultana."

The line went dead, and I sat back with a loud whoosh. "What the hell have I done?"

"You just made your first order to the harem, *Sultana*," Sidig hissed his disapproval, but oddly enough, he did not argue with me either.

Sidig gunned the engine and pulled onto the road merging expertly into the maelstrom of Dar es Salaam traffic. "Where to next, Sultana?"

"Please, you don't have to maintain the ruse for me."

He shrugged his shoulders and expertly missed the small taxi that had pulled out in front of him. "If you say so, Sultana."

I rolled my eyes, thoroughly exasperated. It was hard enough to lie to Grace, but we needed her if our plan was going to work. "Take me to the medical clinic. Then, we can return to the port."

He raised an eyebrow.

I remembered the clinic they had taken me to when I was first abducted. "If this is an ambush, we may need medical supplies before we're finished."

141

He made a sharp left turn that threatened to throw me into his lap. "Will do, but we are going to the airport, not the port."

It was my turn to be surprised.

"The boat will take too long. We need to get over to the island as fast as possible. Our best bet is to fly."

I swallowed hard and nodded. This sounded reasonable until we pulled up to the airport an hour later with the supplies. "Is that what we're taking?"

Sidig shrugged. "We don't have time for the commercial plane and all the questions that come with it."

"If you say so," My heart sank down to my toes. Being pushed out of a tree was bad enough, but this? I stood in front of a vintage fifties' aircraft. It looked like a flying time capsule. The paint was completely faded, the propellers did not look stable, and the fuselage had its fair share of dents. I shook my head, but then I thought of Amir and ground my teeth in determination. What the hell, if I die? I would still come back to haunt his ass and Sidig's too.

I sucked up a lung full of courage and approached the plane, ready to take the first step into insanity. At least I'd changed clothes back at the clinic. We'd found a spare set of Amir's pants and top in the bag. I had to roll up the waist of the pants and fix the sleeve of the top for it to fit. I'd insisted on changing clothes, and this was the best we could do under the circumstances. There was no way I would go traipsing through the jungle in a long dress.

A man walked around the plane and stopped in front of us. His skin was black as coal, set off by a wicked grin of crooked, pearly white teeth. He wore a flight suit with a faded insignia on the lapel.

He held out a hand. "Please to meet 'cha. The name is Fritz Matsukoi. You must be the Sultana." His voice had a high nasal quality to it and an accent that matched the rest of the people from sub-Saharan Africa, thick with a British clip. He shook my hand in one hard jerk.

There it was again, someone referring to me as 'Sultana.'

Did they telegraph the name over the internet?

"You can call me Angela."

His grin was infectious, and I found myself smiling in spite of the state of the plane. "Will do, Sultana Angela. Welcome aboard my *lil' puddle jumpa*. I call her India Sea."

I nodded, having decided not to correct my name. I'd just about given up on anyone getting it right.

Fritz reached over to shake Sidig's hand. "Sidig, you're a site for sore eyes. Been a long time."

"Good to see you, Fritz." He pointed at the plane. "She's looked better."

Fritz shrugged. "It's almost time for some more maintenance but no worries. She'll hold."

Sidig walked by me right into the plane without hesitation. "Come on, Sultana."

Did Amir get as frustrated with him as I did? I set my shoulders and climb into the plane. "Don't call me Sultana."

143

Chapter 17

Angela

Dear God, I swear if I ever touch the ground in one piece, I will give up ice cream and sweets. I will go on a diet and go to church more often. I threw in everything I could think. I prayed and prayed and prayed.

The flight was frightening beyond belief. We'd gained altitude, bounced around, then rather dramatically, lost altitude. On two occasions I knew our number was up. The plane fell into a steep dive only to recover at the last minute. Fritz talked non-stop and acted as if this way of flying was normal. It was a fifteen-minute flight from hell, and somehow, we managed to stay in the sky.

As we approached, the island spread out beneath us, a blanket of rich green tropical vegetation. Up ahead our destination came into view, Stone Town, its colonial buildings tan and weathered in the tropical sun. I was ever so grateful to survive the flight and made a few extra promises of contrition to God just in case the landing did not go well.

In short order, Sidig rented a Jeep, and we were on our way into the interior. He pulled out his phone and dialed. "I'm letting Grace know we are back on the island."

I nodded, all too aware she could shoot us if we did not give her a heads up. The landscape passed by in a blur hardly registering on my troubled mind.

"Don't worry Angela; we'll make it."

"I'm not sure I believe you. Look at the state of this road."

He changed gears and diverted around a pothole. "They had to traverse another road that's in worse repair and takes them farther to the south than they need to go. We are taking the direct route and will get there sooner."

We moved at a bone-jarring pace, under the broiling hot sun with no air-conditioning. Fields and farmland soon changed to dense brush and then jungle. Yesterday we'd passed through here heading for Stone Town. I was leaving the island, returning to my workaholic life. I never imagined I'd come back determined to save Amir. Two days with him was enough to change my priorities and fly into the face of danger. I could only imagine what the next twenty-four hours would bring.

Sidig pulled off onto a dirt-filled track and drove for another twenty minutes before he stopped. "We're here."

I grabbed my backpack full of medical supplies and stepped out of the Jeep. The jungle rose like a vertical wall in front of us. Impenetrable. Mysterious. A lump formed in my throat.

This was going to be a long walk.

Sidig pointed ahead. "There's the trail."

Dense brush and tangle vines faced us. There was no opening or anything that remotely looked like a path. "Are you sure this is the no-shoot-me way into the compound?"

He hefted his machete and swung at the mass of vegetation in front of us. "Yes, I'm pretty sure."

We forged our way through brush, climbed over thick roots and under low branches. Insects buzzed, eager for our exposed flesh. I was thrilled I'd changed into pants and a shirt—there was less exposed skin for them to nibble. The jungle was alive with sound; birds whistled and chirped, animals ran along the tree limbs, leaves quaked and rustled in the afternoon breeze.

We made steady progress until Sidig stopped. "We've passed the first guard." He raised his chin slightly and made a whistling sound finishing up with clicks that seemed to emanate from the back of his throat.

Something that sounded like a bird made an answering call. Sidig grunted and started to walk again.

Less foliage covered the ground, and a narrow trail appeared. Sidig's pace increased "The forward guard gave us permission to continue."

I remembered Amir whistling before he entered the cabin after we ziplined over the river. Those whistles meant something. "Are you communicating with them using whistles and clicks?"

"Yes."

A heavy branch blocked the path. Instead of cutting it, Sidig crawled under and entered a clearing with a stout wooden wall running through its center. "Welcome to Sultan's Harem."

"Oh my God. This is amazing," I was breathless at the sight before me.

The wall was ten feet tall. Women were stationed on top pointing rifles at us. Behind them the canopy of a central tower was visible. Its roof camouflaged to look like the tops of the surrounding trees. Two women materialized from either side of the jungle pointing spears at us. They approached cautiously, clearly studying us, looking for signs of danger. "Um, you're sure we came from the don't-shoot-us side of the jungle?"

Sidig winked. "Yes, Sultana." He faced the advancing women and whistled two sharp tweets, then two short tweets. "If we had not, we would already be dead."

The women lowered their spears and stopped in front of us. In this instance, I understood the importance of body language. I squared my shoulders and lifted my chin, attempting to communicate my lack of fear and my right to be there.

Sidig spoke to them in Kiswahili. He motioned toward me and said the name, 'Sultana.'

The ladies gave me a hard looked then finished their conversation with Sidig.

"They said you may come in," Sidig translated.

The taller woman wore a leather vest and jeans and had a metal armband around both arms. Surprisingly, cornrows zig-zagged across the crown of her head, just like mine. The only difference were the bright blue beads woven through the middle row. She bowed. "Sultana, I am Grace." She motioned toward the other woman. "And, dis is D'jana. Welcome to the Harem."

D'jana wore the same outfit and hairstyle except her beads were green. I wondered if this was where Amir learned to braid hair.

I returned the bow. "Thank you so much."

Grace spun on her heels, and we followed her to the harem.

*****

A_{mir}

We stopped for a third time in as many hours; the road an impossible quagmire of ruts and pits from the storm damage. One section, where the road was completely washed out, Mustapha made us get out and walk around while the driver took the truck another route. We met up with the truck sometime later. They deliberately kept me from speaking with Olanda. She was indeed up in the front cabin guiding them to the southern entrance.

Dread grew in the pit of my stomach even though I knew the compound had the firepower and well-trained staff. There was the distinct possibility I would not make it out alive. My only regret was not seeing Angela again.

I told her I loved her, and I meant it. She made me stop and listen to her; something I only did with the women in my family. She was all at once exasperating, opinionated, brilliant and bold. She was firm in her beliefs and had no problem expressing them. I expected her to go along with my idea for rappelling into the trees, but, she had something to say. The fire of her indignation could've fuel twin suns. I found myself basking in her glow, ready to lean into her and burn for an eternity.

Her passion for medicine was deeply ingrained in her soul, the care she gave Maritsa was complete and uncompromising. Even when Maritsa let it slip she'd been listening in on us, Angela did not waiver. She was compassion wrapped over a spine of steel. Exactly the kind of woman who could grab my heart and own it.

Sending her away tore me into so many pieces it would take a lifetime to put them back together. At least she was safe on a plane heading back home well out of range of this madness. I tensed my fist, wanting to hit something, yell and scream because we would not be together. I wished... Well, I wished a lot of things, but most of all, I wish we had had more time.

The truck stopped abruptly. Mustapha got out of the cab and came to the back. "Everyone, get out."

Talima scrambled out ahead of me. She saw Olanda and tried to run to her, but Aubrey stopped her. The child squealed and kicked, but he held her tight. Olanda stepped toward them, and Aubrey pulled out his gun. We all stopped moving.

Ephrim grimaced. "Father, he doesn't need to be so rough."

Mustapha ignored him and gave us a wicked grin. "I knew you two were smart enough to know when you were beat." He pointed toward the jungle. "Now, lead us in Amir and no funny business. I want what you stole from me."

So far the plan was working. He did not know we were leading him into a trap. I looked around. "You are going to march thirty women out of here?"

He shrugged. "Not that it is any of your business, but I have another two trucks coming to this location to carry them out of here and to the port."

Grimly, I led them toward the jungle. Trees towered over me. Ahead, and to the right, a slight gap appeared in the foliage. It was the southern path. The harem had lookouts to watch this area. They would know we were there long before we reach the end. Those men had rifles, but they were walking into unfamiliar territory and going against a compound full of fifty determined and dangerous women.

Chapter 18

*A*ngela

We followed Grace through the gate. The fence towered over us, its interior walls fortified with a walkway that ran along the top. Sentries patrolled there and kept a watchful eye on our progress. We passed women who stared at me like I was an alien but nodded at Sidig in recognition. Children ran up to him with bright smiles on their faces. His normally somber visage produced an open grin. He bent down on one knee to greet them. Sweets appeared in his hand like magic; each child received one then swiftly ran away. Grace waited patiently for them to finish, her stern look softened at their antics.

The central building towered in the middle of the area. Its wooden walls were painted a dark green like all the other homes in the compound. They blended naturally into the jungle, which was left to grow unchecked between them.

"Did we get here in time?" I asked after we entered.

"Yes," Grace said, offering me a seat. "We have been monitoring our perimeter ever since we got your call earlier today."

"Good, then there is time to prepare. I brought medical supplies in case we need them." I showed her my backpack.

Grace folded her arms and gave me a hard stare.

Uh oh, here it comes.

Now, she would challenge my identity.

"Thanks for *de* supplies. I have one question for you Sultana. How is it *dat* you wear *de* braids of our security group?"

Knock me over and tickle me with a feather.

I did not see that one coming. Was I wearing the braids of security? Amir had braided my hair last night.

Oh, that's right, he hedged a bit on his answer…

He'd watched a lady from his *harem* braid hair. Ha! I knew I would figure it out.

I must have taken too long with the answer. She cleared her throat. "I do not mean to question the Sultana, but we have certain codes of conduct here."

I reeled my mind back in. There was no way I would let her know Amir did my hair. He probably did not even realize there was a hierarchy of braids here in the harem.

Go with the fib, kiddo, DC Angela chimed in.

"I don't mind. I fell into the lagoon the day before yesterday and my hair, well, it needed a re-do. One of the staff offered to braid it for me. I admired her daughter's hair and asked she do mine like hers."

Sidig cut his eyes at me. My hair was not braided when we arrived at the retreat after swinging through the jungle. Matter of fact, it wasn't when we went to the hotel. But it was done after I spent the night with Amir. I lifted my chin and looked him square in the eye, daring him to say something.

She grunted. "Oh, I see."

I could tell she had more questions, but her phone chirped; she pulled it out to read the text. "*De* trees prevent strong cell receptions, but text seems to come through fairly well. *De* southern lookout just spotted Amir. He is wit' Olanda and six armed men. *Dere* is a child with them. *Dey* are not sure, but it could be Talima."

*****

*A*mir

The path was normally overgrown with dense brush. The storm had made its condition even worse. Bugs and mosquitos swarmed in thick groups. Every few steps the men would curse and slap a piece of exposed skin. I smirked in satisfaction; the bugs would be more voracious the farther we trekked into the jungle. At least Talima and I would not be as severely bitten. The women had discovered a natural repellent they mixed into all their oils and hair products. Olanda faithfully rubbed it into Talima's hair and skin every day.

As we continued, each step was punctuated with a slap and a curse. Sweat ran freely down the men's faces, their shirts stuck to their backs. Leaves and underbrush produced a soggy crunch with our passage. These men made more noise than howler monkeys after a leopard invaded their trees. Security for the compound could track us blindfolded with the noise these idiots were making.

Two of the men moved ahead using the machetes to clear the path. Our progress was slow and laborious. I offered to help, but they did not want to give me a weapon.

Go figure.

It took well over an hour to reach the outer perimeter. Through the trees, I could see the wooden walls of the enclosure. Sentries were in the trees watching our progress, but let us go by. Their tweets and whistles of communication echoed through the air. The message was clear; they wanted me to turn off the trail. Leave the path, and they would let everyone live. Stay on the path, and they would follow my shoot to kill directive.

That was what I wanted. We needed Mustapha eliminated for good. I forged ahead.

I had to get Talima away from our group for her safety. "Mustapha, you don't need the girl. Let her go."

"You think me a fool? I will not let her go until I see the compound."

"The compound is heavily armed. I don't want her injured."

"Bah, those men who are their security will cut and run just like the ones who originally let us take them."

I had news for him. These were trained women, and they were going to make a stand. No one in that compound would throw down their weapons and run. I kept going a few more steps and a gun fired. The bullet hit the tree above my head with a *phttt* sound. I stopped.

They had missed deliberately.

What portion of shoot to kill do they not understand?

Talima yelled, "Sultan." She kicked Aubrey, bit his hand, and he released her.

Olanda shouted, "Talima, run for the burro."

Instead of running to the small cave we taught the children to go in times of danger, she ran to me. Instinctively, I bent over to scoop her up, just as another volley hit the tree right above my head. She clung to me like a second skin. I could not get her to release me. "Talima, sweetheart, you must let me go."

She shook her head. "No."

I ducked down to keep her out of the line of fire. I was fairly sure they would stop firing when they saw her, but I decided to be cautious.

Suddenly, the air was alive with whistles and tweets. We were surrounded. The compound came alive with war cries.

*****

155

*A*ngela

"I order you to stop shooting!"

Grace had taken us to the fence. We climbed up to watch the progress of the group of men who were coming our way. Amir was in the lead. He would appear then disappear behind the leaves and tree trunks. I heard the click of the rifle and looked over to see one of the guards aim. My command came too late. She shot at Amir. But, the shot hit the tree above his head.

"What the hell are you doing?" I demanded.

Grace swung around and glared at me. "De security of this harem is my responsibility."

I waved my hands around, my voice loud and raspy. "Warn him at least."

Grace pointed at Amir. "What do you think that shot was? She could have hit him."

In my wildest dream, I never guessed I would be in this situation a week ago. Standing in a compound yelling at a woman to keep her from shooting the man I love.

Oh yes, I love him, and I would move heaven and earth to save him.

"I am the Sultana, and I say we whistle or tweet or make smoke signals, but we tell him to get out of the way. Then, you can shoot whoever you like."

Grace gave the woman with the rifle a signal. "Another warning shot."

The woman aimed at Amir.

"No! You may hit him." I jumped toward her, but Sidig caught me.

"Be careful; you may fall."

"Let go; I love him, and I have to stop them," The words came out in a panicked jumble. He was so surprised at my declaration that his gripped faltered and I almost fell off the edge.

Down below, Amir waited at the edge of the jungle. He stood there stoically knowing what was coming. A pale-yellow streak of gold ran up and jumped into his arms.

Grace yelled. "Wait."

It was too late; the woman had already pulled the trigger. But, she must have seen the child also. At the last second, she raised the barrel a scant millimeter causing the shot to go high. It hit the tree above Amir's head.

I was tired of guns aiming at him and began throwing orders around. "Get down there. Draw the other men out. We have to give them a chance to get away."

Grace was smooth under fire. "You heard the Sultana; sound the alarm. Move!" she translated it into Kiswahili. As one, the women in the trees, and in the compound, whistled and tweeted. It felt like their collective will rode up into the air on the power of that sound. I ran down the steps toward the front gate.

Chapter 19

*A*mir

The war cry of the women was designed to incite fear into the hearts of any who heard it. From the looks of Mustapha and his men, it worked. I used this distraction to put Talima down and push her toward the burro. "Talima, run and don't look back. I mean it."

Her eyes were as wide as saucers. "Yes, Sultan."

She let go of me and ran through the trees. Aubrey muscled forward in pursuit. He stopped short when a woman dropped out of the tree and tackled him. They went down in a heap.

Olanda spun and hit the man to her left. I went after Mustapha. He raised his gun. A rifle fired and the gun in his hand flew away, hit a tree and broke apart. He yelled and grabbed his hand. "Ephrim, come help me."

Ephrim hesitated then pointed in the direction I sent Talima. "I'm sorry, Father. Aubrey is after the girl. She needs help."

Through the trees, ran a streak of a yellow. Aubrey lumbered after her. Behind him lay the inert form of the woman who jumped him from the tree. I knew Ephrim

158

was a good man, and I did not understand how he got tangled up in this operation. But, Talima needed help, and he was the closest help she had.

"Go help her," I yelled.

Ephrim bolted in her direction. I was distracted enough that Mustapha charged me, and we both went down in the bushes and tangled in the undergrowth of the jungle.

"Amir!"

Was that Ahnjela's voice? I shook my head. *No way was that her voice.* I concentrated on landing as many blows as I could on Mustapha's head. I rolled over and threw him off me. We battled it out, slipping in the damp foliage. Vines and tree limbs prevented either of us from gaining the upper hand in this fight. I stood up and went on the offensive charging him and pushing him into the stump of a fallen tree. He grunted when his back made contact. Then, he flipped me over, and I fell into a neighboring tree. The impact caused my head to ring like a gong. His foot twisted on a vine as I came at him again. We both tumbled out into the clearing in front of the harem.

I threw a left jab that connected. He shook his head, spun around and threw a right hook to my gut knocking the wind out of me. I grabbed his right arm and twisted, dislocating his shoulder. He screamed in pain and hit me in the eye with his left. I fell back.

A shot rent the air. We both stopped, out of breath, winded. There stood Angela holding a gun, smoke curled from the barrel in a white vapor. I wiped the sweat from my face in an attempt to clear my vision. My eyes deceived me. Angela was in the air winging her way home, not standing here in front of my harem with a smoking gun in her hand.

She pointed the gun to the right. Aubrey held Talima by the arm; tears streaked her face, her dress torn to shreds on one side. With his right hand, he aimed a gun at Ephrim who stood in front of them.

Ephrim held his hands up. "Aubrey, put the girl down."

Aubrey swung Talima in an arc. She whimpered.

"Ephrim, you are too soft-hearted. I told your father so. You do not deserve to inherit his business."

Mustapha stepped closer. "What is this I hear? What are you doing, Aubrey?"

"I am taking over. You are old and weak, and your son is a sniveling coward." He pointed the gun at Mustapha.

Mustapha stood his ground. "How dare you? Is this how you repay me for pulling you out of the slums?"

"Call it what you will. Your men said they would follow me if I killed you before they got here to pick up these women." He gestured toward the harem. Angela stood up front; she was tall, proud and in danger. Right where I did not want her to be. I waved my hand to divert his attention. "Hey, give up the harem and leave if you want to live."

His laugh was rough. "I'm killing Mustapha first, then you. You cost us a lot of money this week."

160

The rest was a confused blur of motion. He aimed at Mustapha. As his finger pulled back on the hammer, Talima bit his hand and kicked him. He flung her away and finished the shot. Ephrim, already in motion, jumped in front of his father. The bullet hit him in the hip, and he fell back into Mustapha.

Talima landed in Olanda's arms; she leaped from the brush to save her. With Talima out of the way, Grace was free to shoot Aubrey. The first shot to the head killed him, but she was so furious, she shot him two more times.

Angela ran over to Ephrim. "Lay him down on his back. Let me get a look at him."

Mustapha stared at her in a daze and would not release his son.

Angela shook his shoulder.

He finally focused on her and held his son tighter. "You speak English."

Angela nodded. "Yes, I know. Like an American. Now, put him down."

My head was spinning and my vision narrowed. "Mustapha, let her have him. She's a doctor."

He turned to me. Tears formed in his eyes. "Zahra is not a doctor. How can she help?"

I stumbled over and pulled Ephrim away. Angela scrambled around to begin working on him. "She's not Zahra."

My vision blurred in and out. It began to dim. I sat down on the grass; my head was splitting. Angela worked on Ephrim, but I could tell she wanted to leave

161

him and come to me. She was alarmed by the way I looked. "I'm fine." I pointed to Ephrim. "Help him. He's a good man."

Mustapha nodded, tears fell from his eyes. "He is my son. You must save him."

My vision faded to black as my face met the ground. The last thing I remember was Angela yelling orders and hearing the words, "Yes, Sultana."

*****

Angela

"Someone catch him."

Amir passed out right in front of me. I was putting pressure on Ephrim's bullet wound, and my hands were not free.

"Yes, Sultana." Grace stepped around me and went to Amir's side.

Amir needed medical attention, and I could not leave Ephrim to help him. For one millisecond, I froze with indecision between my duty and saving the love of my life. Then my mind kicked into high gear as I focused on the task. I glanced at Mustapha. He gave me the willies, but I needed help.

"I have to start working on him. Please hold him here." I indicated where I wanted his hand to go. He stared at me for a moment, then followed my instructions.

"Sultana, *de* Sultan will be okay. *De* clinic is coming," Grace said.

Four women wearing white lab coats and carrying two stretchers dashed out of the compound. "What is this?" I asked.

Grace beamed her pride. "We have a fully functioning and fully stocked health clinic."

The ladies set the stretchers down and loaded both Amir and Ephrim on them. Mustapha helped with his left arm. His right arm hung uselessly by his side.

He followed along behind the women but Grace intercepted him. "Sultana, I will *tek* him out and shoot him immediately. *De* others are already dead."

I shook my head. Shooting him sounded like a lovely idea, but if he was Ephrim's father, we needed him as a blood donor. "No, Grace. Put a guard on him and follow me."

"Yes, ma'am." She waved at two other ladies who were dressed like her and had the same style braids. "You heard *de* Sultana. Guard him, and if he so much as sneezes, *keel* him."

I remembered one more thing about their approach to this compound. "Grace, backtrack their trail and erase any evidence of their passage. We don't want their reinforcements to see the entrance to this area.

Grace gave me a wicked grin. "My thoughts exactly."

I had the unsettling feeling she would let some through, so she could kill some more men today.

Chapter 20

Angela

Amir gripped my hand as he came around. He called my name several times, and the ladies of the harem gave me knowing smiles. He'd suffered a concussion when he fell against the tree. The health clinic at the compound was a gift. The medical staff had basic training and were able to follow my instruction without hesitation. Both of my patients were in good hands.

They took care of Amir while I treated Ephrim. Fortunately, their clinic had all the necessary equipment. I put monitors on Ephrim and did a quick workup on him. He needed the bullet removed, and the clinic had a small operating room. I removed the bullet and packed the wound. The rest of the damage would have to wait until we got him to the larger hospital.

Interestingly enough, the hairstyle for the medical unit was individually braided hair with the entire mass tied back in an intricate design using a beaded cord. I rather liked that look and asked them, 'to hook a sista up' while we waited to take Amir and Ephrim to the hospital.

With Sidig's help, we transported them to the main hospital in Dar es Salaam before nightfall.

I sat by Amir's bed most of the night. The hospital had the same antiseptic smells and sounds as those in DC. Occasionally, I walked the halls. My shoes echoed on the tile floor despite my efforts to minimize the noise. Monitors beeped and chimed behind each patient's door. Every few hours, I checked on Ephrim.

Mustapha never left his side. The guy was bad, but he was devoted to his son. How he thought to pass his business on to Ephrim, I would never know. The decision to intervene on his behalf weighed heavily on me. He would be free to continue his slave trade if he chose. I spoke with him, extracted promises on this one point and prayed he would honor his word.

Later the next morning, sunlight streamed through the window, promising another hot and humid day. I called Queisha. She'd missed the safari waiting for news about me. I let her know where I was, and that I was okay.

Amir woke up soon after. He opened one eye then the other and squinted at me. "*Ahnjela, habibi,*" he said in a weak but firm voice.

His bandaged head looked like a mummy; his right eye had a deep purple and black halo around it. Cuts and contusions laced his face and neck. He was a mess, but he was my mess.

"Where are we?" he asked.

"You're at the main hospital in Dar es Salaam."

165

He opened and closed his mouth several times as if he was unsure which question he wanted to ask first. "How?" he finally managed to say.

"We brought you and Ephrim in yesterday evening."

He shook his head and winced. "No, I mean how did we survive? We were way out in the middle of the island." He shifted to ease the pain. "No hospitals out there."

I put my hand on his hand. "The life you save may be your own."

It took him a moment to focus. His grip tightened, and he gave me a weak smile. "I'm not sure what you mean, but I guess you'll elaborate."

I rubbed his hand. It was a simple gesture, but one that telegraphed my feelings far more than words. "It seems you have a *harem*. And, you gave your *harem* carte blanche when they requisitioned supplies for their compound. Because of your generosity, their clinic was well equipped, and I had enough supplies and woman power, to save Ephrim, while they worked on you." I could not hide the pride I had in those women.

I'm sure it hurt his face to smile, but he beamed. "They fixed me up?"

"Yes, and with an efficiency that would make most western clinics blush."

He rubbed his thumb across the back of my hand. "I used the cash I made from smuggling to pay for everything the harem needed. Apparently, they spared no expense on the clinic." He shook his head. "I had no idea."

A few more things clicked into place for me. "The spice business is good but not good enough to support a compound of about fifty people?"

"More like eighty with the children." He gazed at me with those big black, dreamy eyes. "I wanted to tell you about them."

I gave him a sly smile. "Really? It felt like you were trying to hide them for some reason."

"I swear, I did not sleep with any of them. I only protected them," he was so earnest in his declaration. It was all I could do not to laugh. "I told them I didn't want a harem." He was actually shaking.

I cut my eye at him. "Are you sure? They're very fond of you."

He tried to lift his head but winced from the pain. "I'm telling you the truth…" He stopped and stared at me before falling back on the pillow. "Are you teasing me?"

This time I did laugh. "Now, why would I do that? Especially when they were quite eloquent about their relationship with you."

He growled, "I bet Grace was the most eloquent of all."

My fingers tangle with his. "Yes, she was. She told me how you put your life on hold to take care of them and sacrificed everything to keep them safe."

"*Ahnjela*, habibi, if all this sacrifice meant meeting you, I would do it again." He brought my hand to his lips and gently kissed it. An electric thrill ran up my arm and straight to my heart.

167

I beamed. "You sweet talker. Keep it up and see what happens."

"I plan to," Amir shuddered. "I wanted to protect you, and what happens? I look up and there you were holding a gun and standing right in the line of fire. You nearly gave me a heart attack."

I'm sure I did almost give him a heart attack. My heart was in my throat instead of in my chest the entire time I had been out there. We were quite the pair, the surgeon and the sultan. I smiled at him. He was bruised and bandaged, but he was alive. There was so much we needed to talk about. We had to air out our feelings. Figure out where to go from here. "Amir, I want to talk to you about—"

The door opened, and Mustapha walked in. I jumped up, never feeling comfortable in his presence. He held his right hand up, his left hand was in a shoulder harness, face bruised as badly as Amir's. They'd both pummeled each other severely yesterday. "Peace, sister, peace."

"How is Ephrim?" I asked.

"He is awake and doing much better." He stood at the side of Amir's bed. Amir tensed and lifted his chin in defiance.

Mustapha chuckled. He'd trimmed his beard, and his face was not as dire and menacing. "Peace to you too, brother."

Amir did not relax. "To what do we owe this visit?"

"My son will need another surgery, and the Sultana asked me to stop by and get the names of some surgeons with the expertise he needs."

Amir turned a raised eyebrow my way. "What is he talking about?"

I had told Mustapha I'd treated him to my fullest capability, and they would need an expert for the last surgery. I did not expect him to come find me so soon. "I worked on Ephrim last night. He is doing better, but he will need more surgeries."

I pulled out a notepad I'd borrowed earlier from one of the staff, wrote down the name of a couple of surgeons and handed him the paper.

Mustapha took a moment to gather his thoughts. "Amir, thank you for speaking up to save my son." He looked at me. "Thank you, Sultana. You saved his life, and for that, I am deeply in your debt."

"Honor our agreement and consider the debt paid," I said.

Mustapha grinned. "I have begun the process as you requested, Sultana."

Then he turned and addressed Amir directly, wagging his finger at him. "You have a rare woman here. I can't for the life of me figure out how you found her. But, if I ever hear you made her sad in any way, I will personally find you and gut you."

With that threat lingering in the air, Mustapha gave me a bow, turned and left the room.

Amir sat up. I raised the head of the bed to give him support. "What just happened?"

I shrugged my shoulders. "I don't know. He was pretty clear about the last bit though."

"Yes, he was. He was also clear about referring to you as, 'the Sultana.' Care to explain?"

I sat down on the edge of the bed. Not knowing where to begin nor wishing to rehash everything. I came up with the shortest answer possible. "It's complicated." He tried to interrupt, but I forged ahead. "Besides, I told him not to call me that."

Now, Amir really was confused. "He obviously ignored that request. What deal did you make with him? You know he cannot be trusted."

I patted his hand. "Don't worry. In exchange for saving his son's life, he promised to stop trafficking women. He also promised to pay restitution."

"You got him to agree to that?"

I nodded my head, a big triumphant smile plastered on my face from ear to ear.

The door opened and in walked a handsome, older version of Amir. I quickly hopped off the bed to face him, guessing this was Amir's father. He ignored me and walked right up to Amir.

"Amir, what happened?"

"Father, I'm okay. This is Dr. *Ahnjela* Jones. She pulled me out of the jungle and got me immediate medical attention," he replied in English.

Amir's father narrowed his eyes and looked at me as if he suddenly recognized me. "You look a lot like Zahra."

Oh no, not this again.

I held my hand out to him. "So, I've been told."

He gave me a weak shake. "You're American?"

170

I grinned. "Guilty as charged."

He said something to Amir in Arabic. Amir replied and nodded toward me.

"My son explained to me how you helped him." He inclined his head. "I thank you."

The door opened again, and an elderly man, sporting a long beard and wearing robes, strolled in. I glanced back at Amir because I figured he knew the guy.

"*Ahnjela*, this is the Imam," Amir explained. "He is the religious cleric from our country."

His father introduced me. "Imam Mohamed, meet Dr. Angela Jones."

He gave me a slight bow and shook my hand. I assumed they asked him tp come in to pray over Amir for a speedy recovery.

Boy, was I wrong.

"How is he doing?" The imam asked in heavily accented English.

"He will make a full recovery," I answered.

The Sultan clapped his hands. "Great, call in Zahra. We will wed them before anything else happens."

"Excuse me?" I squeaked.

She is here! Zahra, the real fiancée.

And, he was ordering me to go get her, so they could get married?

Before I moved, the door flew open, and in walked my doppelganger dressed to the nines in a silk embroidered dress and coat; a two-woman entourage followed close behind. They both wore beautiful yellow dresses each with a sash made of the material I had

171

wanted to get for my mother. My stomach twisted in knots. *She had some nerve going back to get that fabric.* A bald, portly man wearing a suit and royal regalia trailed in after them.

Oh, my dear Lord, the chief, and his daughter have arrived.

Zahra was the same piece of work I remembered from the fabric store. She marched up to the bed and elbowed me aside. I almost fell. She spoke to Amir in that same horrible nails-on-chalkboard voice.

My God, she leaned over and patted his face like he was her pet hamster.

I balled my fists ready to deck her, but was grabbed by one of the ladies who whirled me around and pushed me toward the door. I turned to protest, and the second lady pushed me out of the room and slammed the door in my face. I stood there staring with my mouth open in shock. I knocked; no one responded. I turned the knob; it was locked. I balled my fist and pounded on it. "Open the door."

They ignored me.

I wanted to cry, scream, and rail at the unknown powers of the universe. I wanted a Star Wars ion blaster to blow the door to pieces just to show them I could. More than anything, I wanted to tell Amir I loved him.

Somehow, I knew deep down in the pit of my soul that Zahra would eventually show up. But, I honestly thought we would've had more time to talk about our feelings and maybe find a way to be together. With enough time, anything was possible. Who was I kidding? His life was already planned as was mine.

Sidig materialized by my side. I'd forgotten he was waiting in the hallway to talk to Amir. My adventure was now over. I took a hard, shuddering breath and prayed for a small measure of composure. With a tear the size of Kansas hanging out the corner of my eye, I asked Sidig for one last favor.

"Please take me to the airport. I'm ready to go home."

Chapter 21

Washington D. C.
One week later

*A*ngela

A week flashed by, and I was walking around in a fog, going through the everyday motions of life in a busy city. As for work, my surgical schedule had been light, but demanding enough it kept me from concentrating on my emotional turmoil.

I sat in my office staring out the window, ignoring the bustle of the late morning DC traffic. My mind wandered, imagining the warmth of his arms wrapped around me; cinnamon and spice swirling in the air, his voice as he purred my name. Sweet memories of our short time together, to hold close to my aching heart. Eventually, I would have to move on, but not now while everything was still so fresh. So raw.

Queisha pestered me constantly, digging for information about the mystery man who'd ransomed and set me free. Then, if that wasn't enough, he'd changed our economy plane tickets to first class. She was not going to let the subject go any time soon. Whenever we were together, the questions came thick and fast, especially if there was an audience, namely our mothers. I'd ignore her or clamp my mouth shut and walk away. Not the best behavior, but the best I could do without falling to pieces.

Someone knocked at my door, pulling me from my thoughts. Today, I'd planned on leaving a couple of hours early, but I had time for a short visit. "Come in."

Dr. Tony Drake, the head of surgery, entered, took two long strides and slipped into the chair in front of my desk. He was always high-strung, brilliant and very eccentric. He had a good fifteen years on me yet respected my opinion on the more unusual cases. So, when he opened my office door, I assumed he wanted some advice.

"Hi, Angie. I have a new case." He sat down on the chair facing my desk.

I looked at his hands to see if he brought the file for me to study. They were empty. "Where's the file?"

He waved his hand. "Oh, it's back at my office. This one is very straightforward. There is nothing unusual about it."

I sat back, intrigued. "Um, why did you come by?"

"Well, you see, here's the thing. I'm not used to a patient coming in and requesting a specific surgeon to assist me."

I was at a loss. He knew how to handle patients and keep them happy. Not unless the patient was requesting someone he did not want on the surgical team. There were a couple of names that would fall into that category.

I figured he came to have me weigh his options. "Okay, tell me the situation."

He got up and turned toward the door. "Follow me. You have to meet him."

We marched down to his office, and he opened the door for me. Inside was a man. His back was to me, but I could see he was tall, dark and liked nice clothes. His deep blue suit was tailored and fit him like a glove. His cologne smelled like the first cousin to Old Spice. "May I help you, sir?" I asked.

The man turned around. He was clean-shaven with close-cropped hair on the side. He reminded me of a diplomat, very polished and precise in his appearance. He seemed familiar, but I could not place him. "Ah, Sultana. I hope you are well."

The accent was crisp and very upper class British, but the gravel in his tone gave him away. I was transported back to the dusty truck they threw me in the day they kidnapped me. Only Mustapha had a voice like that. My throat closed and was unable to utter a single word.

Tony nudged me when I did not move. "So, I was right. There's no way you know this guy."

Mustapha chuckled. "The Sultana knows me well enough."

My wits finally kicked back in. "Mustapha, I asked you not to call me Sultana."

He bowed and held his hand out. "Sorry, I forgot. I will remember the next time, Sultana."

I grasped his hand and gave it a weak shake. Tony seemed satisfied and walked around to sit at his desk.

"Have a seat." He pointed at the two chairs placed in front of his desk. "I see you two do know each other. But, why did he call you Sultana?"

"It's just a name." I looked over at Mustapha. "When last we spoke, I handed you a list of surgeons to help your son. I don't remember writing down Tony's name."

Tony gave me a surprised look. "I can't imagine why you wouldn't put me on the list."

"Tony, he is from East Africa. I thought he would want a surgeon closer to home, so I gave him names of some colleagues in Africa and one in Europe." I eyed him. "Besides, don't you need special visas to come here?" With his criminal record, I could not imagine how he got here.

Mustapha shrugged as if obtaining a visa to any country he liked was as simple as ordering a beer. "I did a favor in exchange for a diplomatic pass."

My mouth dropped open. I did not expect to hear this response. "Well then, I'm glad, for Ephrim's sake, you were successful. By the way, where is he?"

Tony handed me the file. I knew it well. The first half of the file were notes I had made when he was in Dar es Salaam.

"He's being prepped for surgery. Mustapha here would like you to assist."

Mustapha leaned closer. "I insist you assist."

I remembered what I had done to get him this far. "Sure, I'm free."

*****

177

SPICE ISLAND

I arrived at my neighborhood five hours later than planned. The surgery had gone well, and Ephrim was on the road to a full recovery. I, however, was exhausted. The ride on the metro was a nightmare. I swear it transported the entire population of Washington DC on one train. Every stop we made was slow and painful. We reached my station after many delays. Above ground, the hot, humid late afternoon DC heat threatened to suffocate me and turn me into a puddle of sweat. The July weather was nowhere near as humid as Tanzania, but it was bad enough to make my clothes stick to me in private places. I'd decided I did not want to mentally process another thing tonight and was due a bottle of Chardonnay and a luxurious bath.

In. That. Order.

At our local store, I picked up my bottle and some other items before continuing to the house. It was a brownstone nestled in the middle of a typical Washingtonian block. Cars were parked bumper-to-bumper lining each side of the street. Some homes had grass in the front, others did not, each house reflecting the character of its owner. As always, the background noise of a big city hummed in the evening air.

I carried the small bag of groceries up the steps to the house I shared with my mother. Inside, familiar aromas and sounds greeted me. Beef stew simmered in the kitchen, and it smelled like cookies just came out of the oven. My mom was in the dining room on the far side of the house chatting with her sister, Val, and Queisha. I *really* did not have the energy to talk to them. So, I tiptoed into the kitchen to put the groceries away. A fresh baked cookie cooling on the baking sheet made its way to my mouth.

Nothing like emotional eating to end the day.

One long stem glass from of the cabinet, along with my chardonnay, and I was on my way to the back steps.

"Angie, is that you?" My mother's voice floated in from the other side of the closed dining room door. Why were they in there and not in the TV room?

Sheesh.

"Yes, Mom. I'm home. I'm going up to my room, now." I didn't dare open the door because they would trap me in whatever lively debate they were having.

"Can you come in here please?"

I exhaled in exasperation. "Mom, can it wait? I've had a long day, and I'm going to bed."

"Angela Marie Jones, get in here!"

She used my full name.

I closed my eyes and counted to three.

I hate when I get caught. I've got to learn to be quiet when I come home this tired.

I sighed in resignation vowing to make this quick. The wine and the glass went back on the counter. "Okay, Mom, I'm coming."

Our dining room was long and narrow, the kitchen door opened into the space at the far end. There was a spray of roses sitting on the dining room table. Their perfume filled the air along with a touch of cinnamon. I stepped right up to the table and stared at them. Mom stood there in a comfortable housedress and apron. Aunt Val was next to her in jeans and a t-shirt, her arms were crossed and a smirk plastered on her face. Queisha was Queisha, complete with a large gold hoop running through the piercing in her nose, tight-fitting cotton dress and smacking chewing gum. All of them had their eyes trained on me drilling boreholes into my skull.

"Did someone send you…" I did a quick count of the roses. "Two dozen roses?"

My mom handed me a card. "It's four dozen roses, and they are for you."

Spelled in beautiful cursive on the front was the word 'Sultana.' It smelled of cinnamon, spice and musk.

My hands trembled. "There is some mistake. My name is not Sultana."

"Hmm, I thought the same thing. Then this box arrived right after the flowers."

She passed it to me. A diamond and sapphire ring nestled inside a small satin pillow. The last time I saw it, Maritsa had held it in her hand. My name was spelled in neat letters on the top of the box.

Oh Lord, I could not handle this right now. My mother, aunt and cousin were standing there like the holy inquisition. I just had one hell of a day and honestly, I'd left all of this behind me in Tanzania. "Right, um, I'm going to go upstairs, now." I slid the card on the table back toward them. "I'll deal with this in the morning." I slid the box back across the table. "I'll deal with this in the morning too."

Queisha, the smart-ass, piped up. "What about the man that came with the box? Are you going to deal with him in the morning too?"

I opened my mouth to say, 'yes' then stopped myself. Did she just say a man came with the box? I realized the smell of cinnamon, spice and musk did not come from the card. It was in the room. He was standing right behind me. The door must have blocked him from my view when I walked in.

Heat from his body came off him in waves. My buns perked up; he was nice and toasty. That damned DC Angela was panting and preening. Rational Angela licked her lips in anticipation. I stiffened my back in spite of those two, determined to keep my resolve.

"*Ahnjela,*" he said my name slowly emphasizing the 'Ahhhn' and 'Jelaaa.' My knees got weak.

I looked straight ahead at Queisha. Amir was married by now and totally off limits. Tears filled my eyes, my throat tightened. "To answer your question, I will deal with the man who came with these things in the morning too. He can leave, now."

Queisha shook her head and glanced at Aunt Val and my mom. "Oh no, this is too good. We wouldn't miss this for the world. You have been moping around ever since we returned from Africa. And, if he is the reason, then I see why you are moping. Girl, he's fine." She licked her lips.

Oh no, no, no. This had to stop right now. I spun around. "Amir, please leave my…" The word 'house' died on my lips. My man-mountain stood before me, tall,

181

tan, hard body, broad shoulders, and smoky bedroom eyes. Damn, he fit his light grey suit like nobody's business. I had the urge to lean in and inhale his cinnamon spicy goodness. I would not be able to resist him if he smiled.

Don't smile; please don't...

He smiled. "And, why does the Sultana want me to leave?" His voice was smooth like liquid chocolate. A sinner's treat.

I cleared my throat. "Because you're married."

My Mother gasped.

"Two sentences and it's already gettin' good," Queisha mumbled.

"Do you mind?" I looked at all three of them. They didn't move.

I stuck my chin out in defiance. "Amir, I will not be your second wife."

Those eyes drilled into my resolve at an alarming rate. "Would you believe me if I told you I didn't marry her?"

"But, they brought in an Imam to marry you two. She even had on a wedding dress. Her father was there, so was yours."

He nodded. "Yes, but I told them I already had a Sultana, and I would not marry anyone but *my* Sultana. That would be you!"

Aunt Val moaned, "Oh, he's good."

I ignored that comment and plowed on. "But, you had a business deal with Chief Vintu, Lentu...Whatever his name was."

"Yes, my father and I had a deal with Chief Bintu; I broke the deal."

"Bintu agreed to that?"

"No he didn't agree. I had an acquaintance convince him to take my new offer… in exchange for a diplomatic pass."

I remembered what Mustapha had told me earlier in the day. He did a favor in return for a diplomatic pass. Now, a few things fell into place, especially his ability to bring Ephrim to the U.S. so quickly. "That acquaintance would not have been Mustapha?"

Amir gave me a wary look. "What makes you think it was Mustapha?"

"He was at the hospital today. He'd arranged for Ephrim to have his surgery there."

The look on Amir's face convinced me I was on the right track. "He must have helped you with the Zahra situation by convincing Bintu to release you from the marriage agreement. In exchange for his help, you arranged a diplomatic pass for him to bring his son to America."

Amir chuckled. "I knew he needed the pass to bring him to the U.S. for medical treatment. I had no idea he'd found your hospital," His expression was that of complete surprise.

Mustapha really meant what he'd said about keeping me happy, enough to put their differences aside in order to help Amir out. But, he was a hard man and could've easily roughed the chief up a bit. "Mustapha didn't hurt

Bintu did he?" I put my hands on my hips and gave him my stern I-mean-business look.

"He didn't harm a hair on his head,"

"That's easy enough for you to say," I wagged my finger at him. "The man is bald."

Amir placed a hand over his heart. "I promise. Bintu and Zahra are fine. All I had to do was pay the dowry."

"What? How much?" I held up my hand. "I don't want to know."

He continued, "I also had to leave the island."

"You were kicked off the island?"

He gave me a crooked smile. "Yes."

"You can't leave the island; your harem is there." I stopped myself by covering my mouth, but it was too late. Ol' sharp ears heard me.

"A harem? I want to join," Queisha yelled.

"He. Has. A. Harem?" my mom exclaimed.

Aunt Val, fanning herself, ended it with a "Dear Jesus."

"It's not what you think." They were getting a small part of what had happen, and with their wild imaginations, the story would balloon out of control. Before I could elaborate, Amir chimed in with an explanation.

"She's right. It's not what you think."

"See, just like I told you," I said to the trio.

"The harem now belongs to *Ahnjela*," Amir finished with a wide grin.

That stopped me cold. In some ways, it made perfect sense. The women took my orders and accepted me into their ranks. However, I'd met them once and under severe circumstances, which did not automatically translate into ownership of the group. "No way, I don't believe it."

"Oh, yes way. They stopped listening to me, and they'll only take orders from you."

"When did that happen?" I was flailing my hands at this point.

"It happened the day you called them up and told them you were the Sultana and started throwing orders around."

"I did it to save you," I yelled.

"It worked." He grasped my hands and kissed my fingers. An electric fire dragon snaked down my body and pooled low and hot and mean.

Why did I let him touch my hands?

My engine was now revving and raring to go. He moved closer to me, and I gazed up into his eyes. "*Ahnjela*, marry me."

There was still the problem with him living in Tanzania and me in Washington DC. "I'll not have a long-distance relationship."

He reached over and picked up the box and pulled the ring out. "My father decided I would do better as a diplomat. I am now his attaché here in Washington."

"You're here for good?" I asked.

He nodded and slipped the ring on my finger. I let it stay there. "Please say, 'yes.'"

"I thought you didn't beg?"

185

"You cured me of that little problem." He wagged his eyebrows and closed the gap between us until our lips nearly touched. "I was in love with you from the first moment I pushed you out of the tree."

"You pushed her out of a tree?" My mom asked.

Aunt Val went next. "Why would you do that?"

"Go on and kiss her," Queisha laughed.

Amir laid one of his searing kisses on me. It was hot enough to take my breath away. "Yes, Amir. I will marry you. I was in love from the moment you picked me up and carried me out of the water."

"He can carry you?" Aunt Val asked.

"Is he really *that* strong? I wanna see this," Queisha chimed in.

"Forget about that. I want to know about the dowry," my mom said.

Amir turned to my mother. "Ah, yes, the dowry." He pulled out an envelope from his inside pocket. "This is the full tuition for two of the ladies in the harem's medical unit. They will be applying to your medical program in the fall, *Ahnjela*. I make this gift to you and your harem."

My dearest wish was to have at least two of the women I met at the clinic come to the U.S. to finish their medical training. This was a wonderful and unexpected gift. "Thank you, Amir."

Queisha vigorously shook her head. "Oh no, Boo. I think my aunt was talking about putting some coins in her bank account,"

I swear I could freely throttle that girl. "Queisha!"

"What? I'm just tryna keep it real."

My family was as much a handful as Amir's. "You see what I have to deal with? Which reminds me, where is Maritsa?"

"She is outside in the car. She insisted on waiting out there."

"She's here?" Why was I not surprised? She'd put too much energy into seeing us together and wouldn't miss this for the world.

He smiled and gestured toward the door. "With an extra helping of Nutmeg soup. Just in case I messed this up."

That lady was determined.

"Oh, for heaven's sake." I charged out the door and found a dark sedan sitting by the curb. I had not noticed it when I came home. The window rolled down. Inside, a beaming Maritsa was sitting next to Olanda and Talima.

"Come on in and meet my family," I said.

*****

*A*mir

They all filed in with Angela carrying the covered bowl of Nutmeg soup. Maritsa was so happy she absolutely floated into the house.

I made introductions. "Mrs. Jones, Queisha, Val, this is my grandmother Maritsa, the head of my security Olanda and her daughter Talima. The ladies greeted them with open arms. Maritsa squealed when she saw Angela's mom and gave her the traditional kiss on both cheeks.

Then she started in. "So good to meet you. Angela is a good *gal*, a good *gal*. She glued me up, see." She patted the side of the traditional Zanzibari dress she insisted on wearing to meet Angela's mother.

"Really? What else did she do?" Angela's mother was fishing.

Maritsa beamed. "She *keep* 'im happy in bed too."

Angela raised her voice to get everyone's attention and stall any more embarrassing comments. "Does anyone want tea?"

Queisha waived us into the kitchen. "You two make the tea. I have more questions to ask."

Angela stood up to complain, but I managed to hustle her into the kitchen. She put the kettle on, turned to me and gave my temple a light caress. "How's your head?"

I inhaled her jasmine scent and leaned into her hands. The contact soothed me, a balm for my tired soul. "It's better, now that I'm here with you."

Most of the bruising had faded, but my head would need more time. I was so desperate to get to her; I'd left against doctors' orders. My injuries would heal, but Angela was the only cure for the giant hole in my heart.

"You shouldn't have traveled so soon." Concern was written on in her face.

"I couldn't wait any longer. I missed you so much. Honestly, I was not sure if you would take me back after everything that had happened."

"So, you had Maritsa make some nutmeg soup just in case?" Her smile was like sunshine to me. "This was your backup plan?"

"It was the best thing I could come up with." It was my only plan. I couldn't think straight without her.

She reached for cups and set them on the counter. "What am I going to do with you?" She nodded toward the dining room door. "Now, that I think about it, what are we going to do with them?"

"Not sure, but I'm wrapping you in my arms and never letting go."

I'd waited a week to hold her, and one more moment was a second too long. She was my exotic, brilliant, beautiful Angela, and I loved her more than life itself. My heart had stopped when they pushed her out of the hospital room and locked the door. The fight that ensued was epic. It took all of my negotiating skills and help from friends in high places to be here at her side. Holding her, loving her.

I slowly spun her around to music only we could hear. She finished the turn in my arms and rubbed her lips against mine. "Is that a promise?"

"Yes, it is." I spotted the wine on the counter and picked it up. "Let's sneak off and let them think we ran away."

The kiss she gave me sizzled what few brain cells I had left. She picked up two wine glasses and led me to a set of steps that ran upstairs to a different section of the house.

189

"I downloaded a Queen CD yesterday," she said. Each step made her hips sway in a way that hypnotized me.

I swallowed hard. "Lead the way, Sultana."

Downstairs, in the kitchen, the teakettle's whistle made a lonely cry for someone to come and turn off the heat. I heard Queisha muscle through the door never stopping her lively chat with my grandmother. Her voice floated up the stairwell.

"Thanks so much for bringing the soup. I'll get bowls for us to try some. Why is that whistle going? Hey, where's Angie and Amir?"

Epilogue
Washington DC
Late September

*A*ngela

The questionnaire had sat in my email inbox for weeks. The heading, in bold red print, requested a review on my African Safari.

The safari I missed.

I sat in my new home office staring at the screen. Amir and I moved a couple of weeks ago. It was a cozy brownstone near Embassy row. My office was warm, colorful and inviting. We set the computer up near the beautiful stain glass window that overlooked the garden. It filtered sunlight into a prismatic display of color that helped me relax. This corner was a perfect spot to answer the request, yet my hands hesitated.

"Are you still hovering over that form?" Amir padded silently to my side and looked over my shoulder. "The page is empty,"

"I'm still stuck on the reply. Which one do I use? Fact or fiction?" There were two ways to answer, with me on the fence, unsure of what to type. Either start with having

191

been mistaken for another woman, kidnapped and met the man of my life, or the safari was great, a perfect trip for your bucket list. I typed both replies and deleted them.

This task had languished in my inbox and would have sat there indefinitely, but Mama J was on her way over and was sure to ask about it.

Lord, give me strength.

Amir nibbled my ear and whispered, "Scoot over, I got this."

I kissed him and happily complied. He and I were unconventional in our approach to couplehood starting with his...*my* harem. We chose to move in together months before the wedding. There were details concerning the welfare and new location of the harem as well as wedding plans with a list of international dignitaries. We decided it would be easier to handle everything under one roof. Needless to say, Maritsa, my mother, aunt and Queisha were all about meddling in our plans. I wouldn't have it any other way.

He positioned his fingers over the keyboard and typed the following.

Mama's travel agency is a great place to find the right vacation for those who crave adventure. My trip included a scenic tour of Zanzibar, ziplining through a spice plantation and a night's stay at a Sultan's palace. I highly recommend Mama J. for making your travel plans. She has an uncanny way of picking a unique vacation package suited for your individual needs. Be sure to check out Mama's travel agency if ya just gotta go!

"What do you think?" Amir beamed at his work.

It was nice, honest and sounded very exciting. Forget the fact I was scared out of my wits during most of it. In these few short sentences, Amir's answer to the request far surpassed my feeble attempts at a reply.

"Wow...I couldn't have typed a better response. Now, press submit and kiss me senseless."

"Your wish is my command, Sultana."

END
Spice Island

SNEAK PEEK!

Check out a preview of the next exciting installment of
Mama's Travel Agency Novels,

Queisha's Cove

She quit her job as a courier but is forced to take one last trip.
He's a master of disguise assigned to protect her.
Deception and lies will be their common ground

Prologue

Washington DC, Mama's Travel Agency
Somewhere near the Foggy Bottom Metro Stop

Queisha

"**I**'m done, Mama J, I want out."

My jaw was set and my attitude mean. Mama James
sat across from me behind her antique desk, arms
crossed, long nails clicking a staccato beat. She insisted
everyone call her Mama J. Her dark bronze complexion
was flawless—as usual—making it hard to believe she

was in her seventies.

"Now, Queisha, don't be so quick to leave."

We were in the back office of Mama's Travel Agency. The room was a decent size, but the travel brochures stacked on every open surface gave it a cramped, closed-in feel. Slick, glossy print full of smiling people on vacation stared at me from every corner. They screamed *leisure* and *adventure* and—dare I say it?—*romance*.

I sneered and pushed over the stack teetering on a plush blue chair in front of the desk. They slumped onto the floor in a messy pile of fifty-two-card-pick-up.

"Wow, you are in a bit of a snit." Mama J eyed me warily.

I slid into the now-vacant chair and crossed my right leg over the left. The word *snit* did not even *begin* to describe my mood. Nervous energy coursed through my body. My foot bobbed back and forth to the beat of my heart. I was angry as hell. "How many times do I have to tell you this job almost got my cousin, Angela, killed? My God, she was kidnapped right in front of my eyes, and, when I contacted you about the situation, all you were worried about was whether or not I was able to make the drop!"

She cut her eyes at me and gave me that child-are-you-crazy look. "I told you we would handle it. Besides, it was critical that our operative there in Dar es Salaam receive the intel you were sent to deliver."

And this was why I wanted to quit my side gig as a courier for Mama J and her *acquaintances* over at the

State Department. They'd recruited me to go on the odd trip to deliver packages for their organization, SPINE—a smarmy little acronym that stood for SPecial Investigations NEtwork. It was supposed to be a *different* kind of organization: no spying, intelligence-gathering only. Information was king and they were the best in the business.

As for me, I wanted to travel. Acting as a courier where the job paid all the expenses seemed the cheapest way to go. Besides, who would suspect an African-American woman from the mean streets of DC would be trusted with important documents? The head guy at SPINE said my style of dress would not even raise the slightest bit of suspicion as I moved around the world, doing jobs for them.

I must concede his point; their plan worked outrageously well. Everyone saw gum-smacking, blinged-out Queisha—to the point that they never even considered me a courier for an intelligence organization.

That's right; I carried shit around the world for *spies*.

My last job almost got a close relative killed and they hadn't given one single damn. I don't have many un-crossable lines in my life, but the safety of my family is one of them. Therefore, I wanted out. "She should have never gone with me to Tanzania." My ankle bobbed at a furious rate now. "I'm pissed at myself for playing along with your scheme."

Mama J crossed her arms and clenched her jaw. "What was I supposed to do when her mother approached me hours before you arrived? Tell her no, her daughter can't go because her niece was a secret operative on a mission?" She hissed the last bit out then closed her eyes and held her palms up to the ceiling and hummed. "Namaste. Lord please help me to calm down. Oh, and give this child some good sense while you're at it."

My foot stopped and I stared at her. "Weren't you listening to a thing I said?"

I stood and walked over to the two-way mirror. I could see into the public area of the travel agency, but they could not see me. A couple of people chatted with Mama's employee, Cyndi, about a Caribbean cruise. A woman and her teenager studied a brochure for Cancun. This was a sweet set up—have your operatives receive their assignments at a travel agency that actually book trips for real clients. Too bizarre. Unreal.

Mama J came over to look out as well. "For what it's worth, I was just as worried about your cousin, Angela, as you were. We had our best agents searching for her. Anyway, it worked out just fine."

"Yeah, she got herself out of the problem," I snarled.

"And she gave me a great review to boot," she added.

A great review. I could not believe my ears. There was nothing more to say. I owed them not one thing—not even my loyalty. She was lucky to get my resignation in person. I'd half-heartedly considered texting it to her.

I slung my pocketbook over my shoulders and wheeled out of her office, determined to be done with SPINE and Mama J.

"One more thing before you go."

"What?" I refused to break my stride.

"We found a lead on your brother."

That stopped me.

"I don't believe you," I grated. I'd been lied to about his whereabouts so many times, it would take more than her word for me to even think about believing her.

I focused on leaving the agency and woe to the person who got in my way. The couple saw me and moved before I collided with them. I pushed the door open and ran into a man.

We collided in a *whoosh* of air. I bounced off his thick waist, lost my balance and stumbled toward the floor. Strong hands grabbed me before I landed.

I understood physics enough to know that two bodies could not occupy the same space at the same time, but physics hadn't been my best subject and my sour mood darkened to rage. I shoved the offending hand away, determined to give him a hard time. "Watch where you're going!" I shouted.

Green eyes nestled in a pudgy, freckled face gazed at me. A smile creased his lips, exposing uneven coffee-stained teeth. "I'm sorry. It's all my fault," he said in a thick Bostonian accent.

I knew that voice and the mop of red hair that came with those eyes. "*Carl?*"

Carl Covel worked in the offices across the hall from mine. He was tall, middle-aged, heavy set, and smelled of mints and bubble gum. He always seemed to show up at the same time I took my morning coffee break. Running into him at work was one thing, but here at

Mama's Travel Agency? Gah. *Not* what I needed today.

"Yes, it's me. You're Queisha from across the hall. Did you come here to sign up for Mama J's Caribbean getaway cruise?"

I was so mad about Angela, I'd forgotten all about the cruise. There was no way I would take a free trip from Mama at this point.

I glanced back toward her office. She stood by the door with a smirk on her face.

My back stiffened and I tugged my skirt into place, then hitched my pocketbook higher on my shoulder. "No. I came to give her a review in person." I yanked the door open. "Sorry, gotta bounce."

I was in the wind and off to work to finish my day and, hopefully, cool down. His gaze followed me as I pushed pass him. It didn't matter; he could stare at merchandise he was never going to get.

Be sure to read Queisha's Cove!

SAHARRA K. SANDHU

Also from
SAHARRA K. SANDHU
Daughter of the Missing

*What would you do if you were swept out to sea
...without a boat?*

Astronaut Sarai Mathews knows the end is near when a giant wave rolls in and pulls her from the beach. But something strange happens: she doesn't die. Instead, she lives and breathes...underwater. While in the depths, she meets a man named Jon Luc. According to him, they're both *Gaiians*, a race of beings who are equal parts human and earth spirit. She is descendant from their missing queen who was lost to slavery. Could any of this be true? Is he real and not just someone she dreamt up during the chaotic moments in the water? Find out when you read Saharra K Sandhu's debut novel, *Daughter of the Missing*.

FIRE IN ICE
A GAIIAN NOVEL

Only ice can contain the fire that burns within...

Dr. Martel Da Mar is on a mission to solve the mystery surrounding the disappearance of a glacial lake located high in the Patagonia ice fields of Argentina. An unknown heat source has melted the lake and the runoff of the water threatens towns and villages below. As the leading scientist in glacial hydrology, he knows this can't be dismissed as global warning. He soon discovers there is something in one of the remaining blocks of ice that radiates an unusual type of heat signature. If they could harness the power, it would be a great source of energy for civilization. There is only one problem; this source of energy is coming from the dragon. It is about to wake...and it is not alone.

Available at Amazon.com

ABOUT THE AUTHOR

Saharra K. Sandhu is an award-winning author of paranormal and multicultural romance novels. During the day she is a scientist, at night words flow onto the page like a magic carpet rig the trade winds on the Arabian Sea. She has traveled throughout South America and the Caribbean collecting folklore and Afro-Caribbean stories for inspiration. Her debut novel "Daughter of the Missing" was a finalist in the Harlem Book Fair Wheatley Book Awards. The sequel, Fire in Ice, won the Romance Slam Jam EMMA award for best paranormal/science fiction romance. She currently resides in the South West with her family.

Connect with Saharra K. Sandhu

You can keep up with the adventures of Saharra via her website, Facebook page, her twitter account, Instagram and her Goodreads and Amazon profile using the following links:

Web:
www.saharraksandu.com

FACEBOOK FAN PAGE:
https://www.facebook.com/The-Gaiian-News-790713904381697/

Twitter:
Twitter: @Saharra_K

Instagram:
Instagram: SKSandhu

AUTHOR PAGES:

Goodreads author page:
https://www.goodreads.com/SaharraKsandhu_Author

Amazon author page:
https://www.amazon.com/Saharra-K.-Sandhu/e/B0181D3VFI

Made in the USA
Middletown, DE
29 March 2022